One KILL

N.O. ONE
THE REAPER'S MAFIA CREW DUET
PART ONE

Cover Design – The Pretty Little Design Co

Editing – Encompass Press Ltd

Cover Photo – Chris Brudenell Photography

Cover Model – Sabrina Marzano

Published by Hudson Indie Ink

www.hudsonindieink.com

DEDICATION

For Maggie Day ~ 1962-2023
And for all those affected in any way by Cancer. It's tragic
and life changing, whatever the outcome.
May it go fuck itself on a rusty fish fork.
And may you all find joy in our book world <3
We love you.

WARNING/FOREWORD

We love that you've picked up our books! But please, take the warning here seriously if you in any way shape or form have triggers of any kind. This duet deals with a variety of subjects, miscarriage, stillborn babies, sexual assault, lots of violence, blood and knife play, dangerous role play, stalking, parental deaths, gambling, and we think those are the main ones.

If by any chance you have a specific thing you need to know about, feel free to drop us a message on social media, email us, or visit our website—details for these at the end of the book.

For those still with us... ;)

This first book in the duet is not as heavy on the spice as the second book, but we like to make sure it all feels real and natural. We're not about to stick a sex scene in there if the characters just aren't doing it, ya know? That being said... it's not exactly light on the spice!

We hope we've done J justice. She's a tough cookie that's hard to break.

But then, we do love a challenge...

THE *Escort* SERIES AND SPIN OFFS

NEW YORK MAFIA
heirarchy

THE DON
Marco Mancini

↓

UNDERBOSS
Ray 'The Stinger' Martini

↓

CAPOS
J - Shadow

Tommy - Babyface

George - The Butcher

Eddie - Snake Eyes

↓

SOLDIERS & CREWS

CHAPTER ONE

J

There's something to be said about having a talented tongue fucking your cunt minutes before putting a bullet through the traitor's skull. Some might say it's fucked up for me to play with my food—metaphorically speaking—but, those people can swivel on a rusty knife for all I care. To be honest, I'd probably get off on it...

It's a shame I had to kill him, really. Tino was a handsome man with just the right amount of stubble on his chin, a jawline that could cut a bitch, and a body anyone with a pulse would stare at in awe. And that tongue... fuck! It wasn't exactly an arduous task, having to get close to him at the not-a-request of the New York mafia don.

However, once that final order to take care of business came through from Marco Mancini, the aforementioned don, it didn't matter that Tino was eating me out. He had to die. Brain matter is now splattered all over the floor of Tino's office and there's a little on my thigh, which I wipe off before picking up my black overalls and pulling them on.

Knowing I only have a few hours before any of his coworkers start rolling up here for work, I pull out my phone and send our usual coded text to my crew group chat.

Me: Hotdog's ready.

Someone should be here in the next ten minutes with a van and all the supplies to get this place cleaned up before morning. When any of us are working a job—even if that job is great at giving head—I make sure there is always some form of backup close by because it never hurts to be prepared.

Being a capo of The Reapers is something I never believed could happen when I began working for Marco—the leaders of the different factions of the mafia are typically men—but the skills I possess are second to none, I'm confident in my own abilities, and when the old capo died, I stepped up. Marco didn't even think twice about it, easily accepting me as the new leader of his cleanup crew after just six years of service. I'm now in my seventh year as The Reapers' capo, and at twenty-nine years old, I'm aware of my unique position as the only female capo to exist.

That's just one of the reasons I'm known as The Shadow.

Some people think I don't really exist, that I'm just a tale told to scare them into submission. To the outside world, I'm just another member of The Reapers.

Gotta say, though, I'm a little relieved this month-long job is now over; I may know my way around motorcycles, but cars aren't my forte. Tino's head mechanic was beginning to get suspicious of my "qualifications" to be here, and I was beginning to get pissed off at his snarky attitude.

"The cavalry has arrived! Where do you—niiiice. Clean through the skull." Shoo takes up all the space in the doorway as he stands and admires my handiwork. "Tab's bringing the body bag out of the van."

"Move your ass, Shoo. You're a fucking mountain, you can't stand in doorways like that." Tab, who is almost as mountainous as Shoo, pushes through the door, covered head to toe in what can only be described as protection. He looks like someone on the hunt for aliens with the hooded coveralls protecting almost every inch of him, plastic booties over his shoes, thick blue rubber gloves on his meaty hands, and goggles that don't fit his face.

I'd laugh, except all of this is necessary to prevent leaving any evidence of them having ever been here.

"I'll help you get the body out, then you boys can do the cleanup. You've got about three hours before anyone's due to arrive for work." They don't argue with me.

"Sounds good to us." Tab unzips the body bag, bending down to begin rolling Tino's limp body inside.

Usually, the cleaning up part is something I enjoy. The monotonous scrubbing, the strong chemical odors, the checking every detail to make sure nothing is left behind, they're all things that help calm my frantic mind. Apparently, watching your whole family being slaughtered at the age of sixteen can really fuck a person up. It may have happened thirteen years ago, but that kinda shit sticks to you like glue.

"He's a heavy fucker. It'd be so much more convenient if he could get up and walk himself to the van." Shoo grunts as he lifts Tino's feet into the bag and begins zipping it closed.

"Yeah, Shoo. Just ask the dead man to walk himself outside, blood spilling everywhere and giving us more to clean." Tab's serious face makes me chuckle, his brows raised as if he actually has a point.

"So the part about a dead man walking himself outside doesn't bother you, but him bleeding everywhere and making more of a mess does?" Shoo and I laugh as Tab realizes what he said then rolls his eyes.

"Fuck you both." He flips us the bird, using both hands, before bending to pick up the now-full body bag. I pick up the other end while Shoo pulls the door open for us, checking that all is clear for us to continue outside to the waiting black van.

The engine is running, the driver-side window open, and Fizz is behind the wheel, ready to help the guys make a quick getaway if needed. She's been a Reaper since inception, she's tough as fuck and her driving skills are like no other, but just like any one of us, she has her weaknesses and a helluva past. Mothering us all is her favorite thing to do, but occasionally—like tonight—she likes to go for a late-night drive.

"Hey, Fizz. I'm leaving the boys to it. Need to shower. You got this?" I know she does, but I like to be considerate occasionally.

"Of course. Go. Get yourself gone, Cap." Her hazel eyes crinkle at the corners as she smiles, shooing me away at the same time.

"I'm gone. See ya later, guys!"

Shoo and Tab wave before heading back inside the building to finish the cleanup and I move straight to my baby. My blood-red Harley. I shove my leather jacket on and wrap my black scarf around my neck before sliding on my matte-black helmet and straddling my bike. The engine rumbles between my thighs as I turn the key and she comes to life beneath me. Having a man there is the only other fun alternative to this.

Riding along the Henry Hudson Parkway in the early hours of the morning is something I'll never tire of. To be so close yet so far from the next state over brings me comfort and pain all at the same time—something I make sure to never forget. Especially at this time of year.

For most people, February is the month for love; valentines, Cupid and his stupid fucking arrows. For me, February marks the time I lost everything.

As soon as I get home to my apartment by Bronx Park, I remove my mechanic overalls, stripping down to nothing, and jump in my shower. There were no expenses spared with my bathroom. It's now twice the size it started out as and I don't regret a cent of the upgrade. All totally worth it for the powerful shower and modern fixtures. Scrubbing my body clean, paying special attention to my bloody thighs, I begin to feel lighter. There's something about the scent of lavender that soothes my soul.

It doesn't take me long to dry off and braid my wet hair, then I pull out some clean black cargo pants and a black tank top, quickly getting dressed. The sun is beginning to shine through the window of my studio, so I grab my leather jacket and bike keys before heading straight back out. It'll take me about an hour to get to Newark, and I'd like to be there to get my table before the breakfast rush begins.

I visit once a year. Same date, same diner, no matter whether I'm working a job or not. I always make time for this and the boss is well aware.

The Prudential Center and the Hockey House come into view as I ride down the side street next to the diner. I could use the nearby parking lot but I'd rather keep my baby away from people and their wide-swinging car doors.

Alma's Diner is like a time warp. Everything inside is the same as it was twenty years ago when I would spend every Saturday morning here with my dad and my best friend, Murphy. A sharp pain tugs at my chest at the thought of Murphy, my dad, my mom, and... nope, I'll save the emotions for later tonight when I'm holed up in my apartment alone with a bottle of bourbon. Tears aren't something I generally allow in front of other people. They're a sign of weakness.

"Hey, stranger!" Alma's cheery voice is like pure nostalgia as she greets me and the smells of bacon, sausage, and egg fill my nostrils, making my mouth water.

"Hey, coffee and a full breakfast, please." I'm polite, I smile, nod my head, but I don't have the capacity for much else as I head over to my favorite booth in the far corner of the wood-paneled space. The seats are covered in a deep-blue faux leather, and the tables are made of the same deep wood as the walls and floor. It's not your typical diner, but it's by far the best one in all of New Jersey.

I know Alma isn't offended by my behavior. She's known me longer than any other living person, but by the way we interact, nobody would ever realize. She moves a lot slower these days, but she'd never give this place up. It's her pride and joy, owned and run by Alma and her husband, with local kids waiting tables during the busier periods over the holidays.

Like every year, I concentrate on the task at hand. I sit in this booth, write on this same diner's napkin, and apologize for my past sins over and over again.

"Here's your coffee, sweetie. I'll bring your breakfast out as soon as Hank's finished frying up your bacon." Alma winks as she places the huge mug of coffee in front of me before walking away and I inhale the fresh scent.

It's hot, but not boiling. One of the perks of Alma's coffee; always at perfect drinking temperature as soon as it's served. None of this waiting for it to cool down crap.

A shadow that isn't Alma's falls over my table and I take a deep, calming breath before folding the napkin, sliding it in my back pocket, then looking up to find a young blonde girl standing there, twiddling her fingers. Confusion and something I can't figure out crosses her features and she looks like she's gearing up to say something.

"Spit it out, Kid. I'm trying to enjoy my coffee. *Alone.*" My voice is firm as I try to hide my annoyance at being interrupted.

"You're her... Jordyn, yeah?"

Woah, nobody's called me that since...

"I'm your daughter, Hallie."

CHAPTER TWO

J

"My name is Hallie." I'm staring at this girl who is getting more and more impatient with my silence by the second. Her growing annoyance is clear in the way she punches her little fists on her hips and cocks her head to the side, giving me a look that could make grown men wilt.

"I heard you the first time, Kid. Sit down, you're giving me a crick in my neck."

"Well, I couldn't tell since you didn't answer. I thought maybe you were getting hard of hearing." I push down my urge to chuckle at her snark. I like it but now is not the time to indulge her.

"How old do you think I am?" My gaze follows her movements as she slides into the old faux-leather seat and crosses her arms over her chest. We're having a wild west moment as we size each other up.

"Old enough to have abandoned your daughter." My gaze narrows, eyes turning to slits, as I try to scare her into submission.

"I'm sure you are a lovely kid." *A bit too bold for your age,* but I don't tell her *that.* She's going to need all the bravado and self-confidence for her adult years. "But, I don't have a kid and I sure as shit didn't abandon one, and if this hypothetical kid knew anything about me, she wouldn't dare make that kind of accusation." Speaking through my teeth, I add a small smile to ease the sour words she now has to digest.

There's a pause in our conversation, her brows slanting in confusion and the corners of her mouth falling with disappointment. I'm watching every detail on her face, from her hazel eyes that seem to change color with every emotion that crosses her features to her slightly upturned nose and her long, long blonde hair falling almost to her waist in thick strands.

I mean, I get it. She could definitely be my daughter... if I'd had one.

"So, your name isn't Jordyn? And don't lie to me. I saw the shock in your eyes when I called you that earlier." I have to admit, her knowing my real name is a mystery. I haven't been called that since I left my dead parents in a pool of blood and ran to Marco Mancini for help.

"It is and yes, color me surprised." I'm trying not to make this a big deal. I don't want to give this girl false hope.

"Well, aren't you going to ask me how I know your name?" Oh, she's getting bolder by the second.

"Does it matter?" Fuck, I really do need to know, though.

She just shrugs like she has a secret and knows I want it.

Okay, I just need to assess the situation like any other and fix the problem. This is literally my job... assess and fix.

"Look, Kid, I know this must be hard to hear and I'm sure you did all this research that ended you up in this place..." I look around the diner. The odds of her landing in this place are slim, but hey, maybe she saw my blonde hair and thought, "Oh! That's my long-lost mother." Who the fuck knows? I've seen weirder shit in my life. "But I can assure you I'm not your mother."

"That's not what my dad said." My back goes ramrod straight and my eyes quickly roam the diner once more, thinking maybe I'm being set up for something. Maybe this kid is a lure and I'm about to get a bullet in the head.

Fuck, I do not want to die in this place, on this day, of all fucking days.

I keep my calm once I take a good look around and find no plausible threats.

"And who, exactly, is your dad?" It's my turn to lean back in the booth and cross my arms.

I don't know what I'm expecting. Maybe she's going to splutter some celebrity name or a dude she looked up on the internet or maybe—

"Murphy Gallagher."

My ears are assaulted by a loud ringing, my mind swimming with reels and reels of memories flashing by as I try my damnedest not to react to the fucking nuclear bomb she just dropped on this mom-and-pop diner.

"That's my dad. His friends call him Murph." I can see her eyes searching my face, trying to find a reaction. She won't because I've schooled my features into neutral nothingness, something I perfected before I even learned how to drive.

"He's your age? Brown hair, brown eyes?" Her shoulders slump as her confidence dies a slow death and it's killing me to be the one taking away her strength. "You were the love of his life."

I don't want to, and I fight it as hard as I can, but those last whispered words punch me in the lungs, forcing the breath I've been holding to rush out from between my lips.

"I knew it!"

"You don't know shit, Kid."

Her spirit and defiance back in full force, this kid—Hal-lie—sits a little taller, her chin a little higher, as her lips spread into a cocky little grin.

I haven't heard Murph's name in over a decade, not since I bolted from my house. I guessed he'd be pissed off that I took off without telling him but I knew I was in danger and putting him on my parents' killer's radar wasn't an option. To save him, I had to become invisible. A shadow.

"I know that... one,"—she plants her elbow on the table, showing me her index finger as she counts—"you can't deny biology." That same finger points at my face then hers and I'm guessing the fact we do share some features is weird.

"I have blue eyes, smartass, so that's not helping your point." I raise a brow, taunting her, but she doesn't waver.

"Dad has brown eyes, mine are hazel so a mix of you two." Her grin grows and I want to laugh at her reborn assurance and that realization makes me pause for a second. Today is not a day where I can laugh, yet here is this complete stranger making me forget the most horrible memories of my life.

"That's not how it works, you know…"

"Close enough."

I shake my head because she's obviously bull-headed and I'm too curious about her other points to stop her now.

"You ladies doing okay? Would you like something, miss?" Alma doesn't show it much but she's just as surprised to see someone sitting at the table with me as I am. I've been coming here as some kind of penance for the better half of my life, same day, all day. It's my remembrance, my break from life and death. The day I allow myself to think about my parents, their death, so much death and blood, my vengeance. Every year is the same. Every year I eat, drink, think, in this very spot until I go back home and cry. Let it all out for the next three hundred and sixty-four days.

And yeah, I think about Murphy Gallagher. The way I abandoned him after… fuck. I can't go there. Not right now. Not with my mind spinning with this weird situation.

This kid is fucking up my routine and I'm not even angry about it.

"Um..." Hallie's gaze darts to me and for all her assurances, she suddenly looks so young without all the bravado. "I didn't have this part planned."

Cocking my head to the side, I realize that, in this moment, she was expecting me to shoo her off and now she's just winging it.

"Get whatever you want." I'm not going to let her starve or whatever.

"Just an orange juice, please." I watch her as she orders. Her profile is so familiar and I can see the resemblance to Murphy. It's in the plump lips and her big round eyes that can't seem to hide an ounce of emotion.

"Sounds good, sweetie. Be right back." Alma leaves, and when Hallie turns back to me she notices I'm staring at her.

"You see it, don't you?" Her question catches me off guard.

"See what?"

"The resemblance between us."

"I see your father, that's for sure."

Then it hits me. The math of it all slaps my brain and shakes the shock right out of me.

"Wait a fucking minute."

"Ah, there it is. Dad said you were sharp." I ignore her sass and search her face for clues.

"How old are you?"

Hallie doesn't answer my question. A deeper, darker, voice echoes from right behind me and sends a jolt of pure electricity throughout my entire body.

"Thirteen. Today is her birthday."

CHAPTER THREE

J

Pain ricochets through my heart as memories of him—of *us*—fill my mind at the sound of his voice alone. Thirteen years of trying to forget the most tragic day of my life suddenly feel like mere minutes as I remember everything I pushed into the deep recesses of my very soul.

It's impossible though.

She can't be...

"I can see the wheels turning, Jaybear." There's a hint of sadness in his deep brown eyes, and all I can do is stare at the man I once loved. My insides are rioting, but on the outside I'm the picture of calm as I fold my arms across my chest and quirk a brow.

"What the fuck is this, Murphy?" Anger. That's how I'm choosing to approach the situation because I don't know any other way to avoid what I'm praying isn't the truth.

"Can I sit?" He gestures to the booth, the navy-blue sweater he's wearing tightening over what is now a much firmer chest than I remember.

"Would you walk away if I said no?" Turning away from him, I face Hallie again, her wide eyes moving between us in excitement. Strange child.

Murphy's responding chuckle makes my heart ache again, and for the first time in thirteen years, I let myself imagine what could have been. If I hadn't run away from him, if my parents hadn't been murdered in front of me, if I hadn't been spared because I was pregnant and they lived by a fucked-up code, and if I hadn't given birth among my family's blood to a stillborn baby...

"Scoot over, Hal. Give your old man some room."

She immediately does as he asked and slides across the bench seat, a look on her face like she knows she's done something she shouldn't have done, but she also knows he's already forgiven her. I used to look at my dad like that.

Anger boils inside me at this sick joke, whatever it is. Somehow, the Irish mafia I've made sure to stay the hell away from have found me again and they're using some dirty fucking tricks. Murphy always managed to stay away from all that crap, but it seems he's been pulled right into the middle of my personal war with them.

"I wanted to do this just the two of us first, but someone is as bull-headed as her mother and snuck out first thing this morning." He glances disapprovingly at Hallie, his tone hard at the end, but his features so much softer than I've ever seen them, the love he has for her shining through as she defiantly pokes her tongue out at him.

I'm seriously questioning my sanity because I'm doubting myself. My thoughts are spiraling and I'm suddenly not so sure this is all a horrible joke or a way to get to me.

What if it's real?

I remain silent, taking a deep breath before sipping at my coffee, as if I haven't a care in the world.

"She's always known about you, since she could talk. I wanted to—"

"Hold up. Who's her mother, Murphy?" I really want him to tell me he was cheating on me as teenagers and got someone else pregnant at the same time as me, because the thought that I left behind a dead baby that wasn't dead could very well kill me from the inside out.

"I already told you. You're my mom."

"Hal! Give her a minute."

It would seem he still knows me just as well as he used to. Processing time is something that I've always needed. I'm calm, calculated, and always go into any given situation with a plan, but this... this is all kinds of fucked up.

Murphy's chestnut hair falls into his perfectly chiseled face as he waits for me to react and Hallie huffs beside him, rolling her hazel eyes in a way that makes me smile. For such a sassy little thing, she clearly has respect for her dad.

This isn't the place to be doing this, to be having this kind of conversation, but it's happening and I can't—won't—run away again.

"You want to come back to our place? Do this somewhere a bit more private?" Murphy leans forward, holding his hands out between us as if he's waiting for mine to join them.

Another deep breath and I stand, pulling out my wallet and dropping my usual hundred dollars on the table for Alma. "Did you drive? I'll follow behind on my bike."

"But I didn't get my orange juice!"

"We've got juice at home, Hal. And don't think this means I'm letting you off the hook for running off this morning." She smiles coyly and it's obvious she has him wrapped around her little finger. He smirks and shakes his head as he moves to stand from the booth and I can't help the inhale at him being so close, the scent of engine oil and mint that is still so uniquely him invading my senses once again. "My truck's in the parking lot out front." He gestures for me to lead the way, always the gentleman.

I hesitate for a moment, torn between thoughts of this being an elaborate trap of some kind or believing in the impossible. There's a flare of hope somewhere deep inside me that maybe, just maybe, I didn't lose everything that day.

I choose impossible.

Head held high, I lead the way out of the diner; Murphy and Hallie follow close behind and cross the road over to the parking lot. I watch them walk over to a light-blue Dodge Ram and Hallie waves energetically to make sure I see them as Murphy opens the passenger door for her and she climbs in.

If she's mine... it doesn't bear thinking about the time I've missed, what she's been through...

Shaking my head, I move to the alley where my Harley's parked and slide on my helmet, zipping up my leather jacket before throwing my leg over the seat. Pulling on my gloves because it's cold as fuck, I start the engine and take a deep, fortifying breath. Today is usually my day for mourning what was lost, what was taken from me, and it's just taken a fucking crazy turn, but I'm nothing if not flexible, able to adapt to any situation.

I can do this.

Twenty minutes later, I pull up behind Murphy's truck in a cul-de-sac lined with mismatched houses. There's a small driveway, just big enough for the truck, so I pull up and park on the street outside the single-story cream-colored house.

"This is sooo cool! Can you take me for a ride?" Hallie is already out of the truck and hovering beside me before I've had a chance to turn the engine off, excitement clear in her big round eyes.

"Not a chance, Hal. Come on inside." Gripping her shoulders gently, Murphy spins her and leads her toward the forest-green front door.

I follow, helmet in hand, into the most suffocating environment I've ever seen. Or maybe that's just me. There are photos of Hallie at various ages, of the two of them together across almost every surface, and suddenly I'm not sure I can handle this. The woman who laughs in the face of danger, who blew a man's brains out less than twenty-four hours ago, is afraid of the family life in front of her.

"Hal, can you give us half an hour to talk? Maybe set up that new PlayStation you opened this morning?" His voice is coming from the next room, which I see is the kitchen as I step further inside, and I watch Hallie's shoulders sag.

"Ugh. Fine. But it's my birthday, so don't forget about me."

"I could never, baby girl." She leans into him, wrapping her little arms around his waist, her head level with his chest, and he presses a kiss into her hair before she turns toward me watching like a psycho in the hallway.

"I know you're my mom." She huffs and tilts her chin higher, brushing past me and heading through one of the doors into what I'm assuming is her bedroom.

Kid's got balls.

"Do you still take your coffee plain, no sugar, no cream, Jaybear?" Murphy's voice calls through from the kitchen as if my whole world isn't crashing around me, everything I thought I knew suddenly becoming complete bullshit.

"Yeah." My voice is firm, steady, void of anything that might portray how I'm really feeling, and I step further into the living area, sitting in the single gray armchair to avoid him being able to get close to me.

"Here you go." Murphy enters the room carrying two black mugs and passes one to me. "Sorry about ambushing you earlier. As you can probably tell, once Hal gets something into her head, I have a hard time stopping her. She's a lot like you." He sits on the matching gray sofa across from me, placing his mug on the glass coffee table in front of him.

"See, you keep saying that. But it's a pretty tough pill to swallow, Murphy. She can't be mine." My thoughts are still a jumble of things, trying to decipher what's real while maintaining a level of calm like no other.

"She is. I found her crying in a pool of blood the day your parents were..." He clears his throat awkwardly, a hint of anger in his tone that he's trying to hide as he struggles to find the right words, but there are none.

"Murdered, Murphy. The day my parents were murdered." Snark is my go-to because I'm not sure how to handle the emotions running through me at the thought of that poor baby.

She wasn't dead.

I left her.

All alone.

My heart cracks a little more and the urge to run away is fighting for dominance, but I already made that mistake.

I already ran away from her once.

"Yeah, the day they were murdered. I went to your house to pick you up for our date and found a massacre. Hallie's cries were the only thing that kept me going, Jaybear. The few left from your dad's crew thought you'd been kidnapped and dropped dead in a ditch somewhere after giving birth in the house. I had nothing to live for apart from our baby girl." It's clearly difficult for him to talk about, he's not making eye contact, his hands clasped together, his arms on his knees.

"Then last year, I saw you leaving Alma's. How could you abandon a baby like that, Jordyn?" His hands are clenched into fists and he's physically shaking, like he's holding himself back from jumping up and shouting in my face. And fuck... he thinks I'm cold enough to leave a newborn baby so I wouldn't blame him if he did.

"She was so fucking cold, if I'd have been ten minutes later I—"

"I thought she'd died..." Murphy's head rises slowly at my interruption and his eyes meet mine. Some of the anger I know was brewing there is seeping into something else. Sympathy maybe? "She was so silent... and blue... and I panicked. Leaving was the only way to keep you safe after what happened, I *had* to run. It didn't take a genius to guess that I was part of the hit and with the baby... well,

I didn't think. I just acted. I just... survived. And... "I shrug in an effort to keep any and all pesky emotions at bay. "Calling an ambulance was the furthest thing from my mind knowing the whole fucking system was in their pockets." I close my eyes, settling my rampant feelings, and neglecting to tell him about what my dad had stolen and the reason the Irish had murdered them in the first place.

"You were alone?" Murphy stands and moves over to me, kneeling in front of me, and clasps my hands in his.

His face is so close, his breath almost mingling with mine as we breathe in the sorrowful moment. But it's all too much. I'm not this person. I need some actual time to process the revelations of today, and there's a little girl in the next room who needs to not have a shit birthday with a fucked up assassin in her living room.

Fuck, I'm a mother.

CHAPTER FOUR

J

"If you don't wanna get nailed, stay out of the fucking brothel!" I grunt at the force of the impact of Tab's meaty fist on my chin. That's what I get for not paying attention while in the fighting cage. To be fair, since leaving Murphy's place an hour ago and heading straight to Devon Quinn's gym, my mind has been reeling. Tab doesn't pull his punches, not since I threatened to kick his balls into next year if he treated me with kid gloves.

"That makes no sense." I duck as he comes at me again, his elbow too low to aim properly.

"It was a... what's it called? A play on words?" I jab him in the ribs, enjoying the grunt that follows. "Fuck, that's my bad side. We ain't fightin' for reals, J, no need to take me out cold."

I mumble an apology since he's right, I shouldn't be taking my frustrations out on him. He's not the one who showed up at my favorite diner with news that's been fucking up my brain for hours.

"It's a shitty play on words, Tab." We're circling each other, contemplating the right move, when I hear the familiar squeal of a toddler. Just yesterday, that sound wouldn't have distracted me, but goddamn it, now all I can think when I hear Dante's favorite word, *duck-duck-duck*, as he runs around the cage is... I missed so many years of my daughter's life. Did she have a favorite word when she was just learning to speak?

Next thing I know, I'm flat on my back, heaving my next breath.

"And the Shadow goes down!" I don't bother to turn my head to see who's speaking. The British accent and the cocky tone of it tells me everything I need to know. Devon Quinn, the owner of this gym, in the flesh.

"England get rid of your ass already? Must be a record."

Tab extends his arm, offering me a hand up, and I take it without even glaring at him. I'm usually the one helping my sparring partners up and the fact that Tab, of all fucking people, was able to get one over on me pisses me off.

"Nah, I'm too pretty to kick out." As Dante barrels into his dad, Devon picks him up and throws him high above his head before catching him with little effort and hugging him tight against his chest.

Madelina Mancini, Marco's sister, has been living her best life. An unconventional life, for sure, but there's no denying her happiness. I mean, I can't imagine having three hot men like Enzo Beneventi, Tyler Walker, and this guy catering to my every whim. And when I say I can't imagine it? I seriously cannot.

No doubt their lifestyle is perfect for them; I've never seen Enzo happier and I've known the guy for thirteen years, since he was once Marco's right-hand man. For me though, it seems too constraining, too much responsibility. Too much work.

"Daddy. Fight. Duck-duck-duck."

Kids are fucking weird.

"Come on, bud. Let's get the whole fam together, yeah?" Devon turns to me with Dante still in his arms. "You're distracted. It's not like you. You doin' okay?"

I roll my eyes because he can't seriously think I'm going to unpack my feelings, or whatever, right here in this testosterone-filled space with men who are supposed to be scared shitless of me. Yeah... I don't think so.

"Go take care of your rugrats. I think the twins are beating up one of my men over there." I can hear Enzo giving the oldest of the two directions on when to hit and when to kick. Knowing these guys have this whole family dynamic down pat brings a smile to my face. Some people have all the luck, I guess.

"These rugrats, as you say, are gonna be the death of me." His words are followed by an affectionate kiss to Dante's forehead as the kid's big brown eyes stare back at his dad. Apparently, no one knows who the actual biological fathers of these four kids are.

The twins were the first to arrive a little over seven years ago. Adalee is the oldest by two minutes, followed by Braxton. They're a force to be reckoned with, for sure. I've sparred with them before, just for the fun of it. Their skills are impressive and when they tag team their opponents, they're a little scary. Physically, they look nothing alike. Adalee chooses to have short hair like her aunt River, Marco's wife, while Braxton wears his longer, in a cross between a surfer and a rock star. Blonde, wavy, and messy all the fucking time. While Adalee has her mother's and uncle Marco's gray eyes, Braxton's are more of a forest green; deep and soulful.

My favorite though is Cairo, the middle one. He's only five, but holy fuck. That kid is going to rule the world. I'm pretty sure he's got some kind of genius brain going on with the memory of a thousand computers on constant overdrive. Not once have I seen him enter the cages, but he watches, his sharp blue eyes bouncing from one person to the other like he's calculating statistics and shit. It's weird but also fascinating.

"Daddy!" Dante is bucking in Devon's arms as he tries to get down. Kid can't stay still for more than two seconds. He's cute though, for a toddler.

"How long you guys in town?" They all live somewhere in England but come back often enough for Marco and River to be a constant in the kids' lives.

"A coupla weeks, maybe more. I think Tyler has an idea he wants to investigate." As a former businessman who is now a stay-at-home dad, Tyler Walker is the epitome of the billionaire husband. Or boyfriend? Maybe they're all just partners? Hell if I know, but it works.

"Maybe I'll get to kick your ass then?"

"Doubt it, but you can always dream." He laughs and my lip curls in mock anger. He's bustin' my chops and that's fine. It's what we do.

"Miss J, your phone is vibrating on your bag." My eyes land on Cairo who, at five, speaks like he's fifty. It's weird, right?

"Thanks, Kid." Hopping out of the cage, I realize Tab's already gone and I'm guessing he bolted a while ago. Devon raises his hand in a goodbye as he tries to contain the ball of energy that is his son and Cairo follows behind in silence.

Still watching the middle kid, I grab the phone and look at the screen. Marco called and I missed it. I'm about to get an earful, no doubt.

"Boss?" I question when he answers after the first ring.

"Mind telling me why you're sparring at the gym instead of resting?" I blink, surprised he'd know where I am before remembering he's the head of the fucking mafia. He knows every-fucking-thing.

"Needed to vent, Boss."

"Yeah, well, I need you rested. I got a job for you." Here we go... the work of a capo is never done.

"I'm good, Boss. Where do you need me?"

One of the advantages of having a female capo in a male-dominated world is that when I walk into a room, heads turn.

Tonight, I've got to test the patience of a dozen men trying to make a deal in The City without Marco's presence. He wasn't invited to their little shindig, and because he's not an idiot, he's not walking into the viper's den without knowing exactly who is hissing out the commands.

My presence, however, will surprise them long enough for me to get the job done. But first, I have to look the part.

Red, backless dress... check.

High heels... check.

Makeup... ugh. Check.

Even my hair is up in some kind of bun twist thing I got from an instructional video on the internet.

Knives... check.

Gotta be prepared for every scenario.

My phone buzzes on the bathroom counter and I'm surprised to see Murphy's name flashing on it. We exchanged numbers before I left, promising to keep in touch so we can figure out how to best take care of Hallie's needs.

My maternal instincts are non-existent, but I'm still human and, for some strange reason, I'm having a hard time understanding... any time I think of Hallie, or her name, or see her face in the forefront of my mind, there's a warm feeling that pulses behind my ribcage.

At first I thought I was having some type of heart problem. A heart attack, maybe? Then I realized I'd had fried food as a midnight snack the night before and chalked it up to heartburn.

"I've got a thing, Murph. What's up?" I don't bother to answer in a polite tone. The only person who gets a hello is my boss.

"Good evening to you, too, Jaybear." My molars smash together at the nickname he's insisting on using for me. It brings up way too many memories and... *feelings* that I'm not ready to have.

"Don't call me that. I'm a grown ass woman capable of ripping out your balls." His chuckle makes me groan into the phone. "I'm serious, Murph. I've got a thing. I don't have time to fuck around. What do you need?" Taking out the mascara tube from my very small bag of makeup accessories, I hope and pray it's not all dried up. The last time I used it was for a gala Marco forced me to attend when Enzo bolted to England and I had to stand in as his right-hand woman.

For three years I had to be at Marco's side for any and all events. My ears were constantly on the ground, my intel knowledge was overwhelming, and as much of an honor it is to be the don's most trusted soldier, it was like a prison sentence for me.

Thankfully, during those years, he began trusting Ray Martino, his new underboss, more and more. And once he got a real bodyguard, he gave me a choice.

I chose a demotion back to capo of the Reapers—the cleanup crew—with the condition that I step in for undercover shit when needed. Like an idiot, I accepted since I clearly didn't know what the fuck I was getting myself into.

"Duly noted. Hallie wants your phone number so she can get in contact with you. I told her I'd ask first." He pauses, like his next words are pained. "I didn't want to assume."

Fuck, there goes that heartburn again.

"Assume what? That I'd just ignore the fact that the baby I thought was dead is actually a beautiful, thriving young lady?" My words are sharp but my tone is as calm as the Dead Sea.

"The last time I assumed something, I ended up hating you for years, so yeah, Jaybear, I'm asking you first. You wanna be in our—" He cuts himself off and it's not until he speaks again that I realize why. "Be in *her* life or not?"

Opening the medicine drawer, I take out the antacid and pop one in my mouth. I'm never eating fried foods again.

"Just give her my number, Murph. It's not a big deal, okay?" Fuck, my mascara is a little chunky but it'll have to do. Can this day get any fucking worse?

A little voice inside my head reminds me that my daughter is alive and well, and that should make me happy. It does, but my emotions are so deeply buried inside the darkest recesses of my soul that I don't even know if I'd recognize love or happiness if it punched me in the face and knocked out my front teeth.

"All right then. You gotta answer when she calls though, Jaybear. She's been a teenager for two minutes and it already feels like thirty fucking years of sass and tantrums." I chuckle at that because of course the child that I created would make her parents' lives a living hell. "She reminds me so much of you... every fucking day." His words are low, nostalgic even, and it makes me pause for a second.

"Murph?" His name on my lips is so quiet I'm not even sure I said it out loud. In fact, I don't even know why I said it in the first place. I have nothing to follow it up with.

"Yeah?" The hope in his voice feels like a gulp of smooth bourbon running down my throat and warming my insides.

This is ridiculous.

"Quit calling me that." I hang up, his laughter ringing in my ears. When I look back up at the mirror, I see myself smiling. A genuine, happy smile.

For a second, I contemplate that look on my face. It changes everything about me, taking almost a decade off my features.

Huh. Weird.

Shaking off the moment, I go back to my regularly scheduled program and scowl at myself for even pretending to be anything but a stone-cold killer with zero emotions. Okay, maybe not zero... I do love my boss's wife and her dog, Polo.

Right. Marco. I need to get my head in the game.

Twenty minutes later, my conversation with Murphy is pushed way back in the recesses of my mind as I step out of a taxi, one red heel touching the ground as a valet holds his hand out to me. Time to fuck some shit up.

My knives are holstered around my inner thigh, the blades made of carbon material so it doesn't wake up the metal detectors I know are at the entrance. I look like any other blonde patron, dressed to the nines and ready to spend a shit ton of money.

Except, the only thing I'm here to do is ruffle some overly sensitive egos.

The first thing I notice as I wander around the newly opened casino are the cameras. Making a mental note of their positions, I smile at the one above a door marked "Authorized Personnel Only". I swear, it feels like whoever is behind the camera is daring me to test my luck.

Not yet, Satan. Not yet.

I could probably make a ton of money here. My poker and blackjack skills are on point, but that's not my mission. However, I'm not ready to scream out who I am just yet if the blinking red eyes planted all over this place haven't already figured it out.

I've been here for a good ten minutes now and no one has approached me except for the waiters offering me a flute of champagne from their perpetually full trays.

It would be strange not to have one in hand, so I walk around and pretend to sip once in a while. Drinking from a glass is never a good idea when you work for the mafia. Sure, years ago, no one would have known who I was. They called me the Shadow for a reason, but four years standing next to the mob boss of New York City made my face one to remember. Someone important enough to become a target.

So, no. I don't drink the champagne.

"Miss?" I turn when someone places their hand on my upper arm. My first instinct is to stab the motherfucker for touching me, but then I remember where I am and what I'm doing.

"Yes?" My one-word answer is clipped and filled with venom. Fuck, I hate being touched.

"Your presence is requested upstairs." My eyes fall to his hand that's still on my arm and, without meaning to, I growl. His hand falls away quickly enough that I don't have to cut it off.

Turning to fully face him, I place my flute on a passing waiter's tray and stand to my full height, my shoulders back and my thighs pressing together so I can feel the comforting presence of my knife.

"Lead the way."

Now, this feeling in the middle of my chest making my stomach vibrate, I recognize. Excitement, adrenaline. The smell of a potential kill.

As we near the door from earlier, I look up at the camera and wink. See, motherfucker? I don't need to sneak in anywhere, I've been invited.

Taking my phone out of my clutch as we make our way down too many corridors for my liking, I notice the ten missed calls from Hallie and sigh. Fuck, I've been a parent for less than twelve hours and I'm already failing miserably.

Shaking off the defeat, I place a call to Marco, knowing he'll pick up but won't say a word, before dropping my hand to my side just as we reach our destination.

Fucking finally.

The door opens and I'm ushered in with a wave of the guy's arm.

"Miss." I push down the urge to roll my eyes. So formal.

"J... The Shadow," a heavily accented voice calls out. My head turns to see who's summoned me to the boys' club.

"In the flesh." My tone is bored; my eyes, however, are hawk-like as I study every man present in this large, rectangular conference room.

There are a dozen men, each looking more regal than the last, but all of them smelling like money and mob hits.

"What brings you to our humble casino? Are you a gambler?" Turning my entire body to face the man speaking, his thick Greek accent telling me everything I need to know, I cock my head to the side and grin like I'd imagine a psychopath doing.

"Zavier Galanos. How... predictable."

CHAPTER FIVE

J

"You have me at a disadvantage." Pushing his chair back, he rises to his full height and I grit my teeth when he uses the three or four inches he has on me as an intimidation tactic. "You know my last name but I do not know yours."

Is there some kind of testosterone school where all boys go to learn the tricks of silent misogyny? Like, okay, we get it... you're taller. Doesn't mean you're smarter, you fuckhead.

Unfortunately for him, I skipped school on the day they taught girls how to be shy and demure. Instead of stepping back, which is clearly the show he wants to put on in front of his hounds as they all sit with baited breath, I step *into* him. Our chests are nearly pressed together, the plunging neckline giving him a direct view of my cleavage.

Huh... his eyes stay on me, never dropping to my exposed skin. Well, well... this man has self-control, let's give him a brownie for effort.

Ignoring his question, I cock my head to the side and frown like a teacher chastising an unruly student. "Don Mancini did not authorize this meeting. You..." I straighten to my full height and narrow my eyes, one hand at his neck tie, squeezing. "Are not allowed on his turf without permission." Galanos doesn't even try to push me away. In fact, I'm surprised by the sudden appearance of laugh lines at the corners of his eyes and the genuine smile on his lips exposing a row of straight teeth, white like innocence; of which he has none.

"Marco Mancini." There's no anger in his voice, only amusement as his eyes drop to my hand holding my phone before he cocks a brow at me in question. "May I?"

I shrug, figuring if Marco wanted to listen in on the conversation then he wouldn't mind speaking to this cocksure asshole. As I lift the phone to his face, I lower my voice a mere octave, "Disrespect him and I'll cut off your balls then have them made into a keychain." His face scrunches up, a normal reaction men have to this mental image, and it gives me a great sense of power. Especially since I'm not bluffing and every fucker in this room should already know it.

There are a variety of responses around the room, ranging from surprise to shitting their pants. I don't need to see their faces to know, I can hear it in the gasps, breaths, and semi-silent gulps. Galanos, however, morphs his face into a charming smile and scoffs, with a small shake of his head.

"Don Mancini. Let me extend my sincerest apologies, your invite must have been lost in the mail." His hazel eyes remain glued to mine as he speaks into the phone, like the smug bastard he is.

"Don't insult me further with lies, Mr. Galanos. Be a man and admit you fucked up. You've been caught. If you can admit to that, I'm willing to hear you out." Marco sounds calm and collected through the speaker, but I know him well enough to guess that he's pissed.

The problem is, Zavier Galanos has some out-of-state connections that the New York mafia would ideally like to stay on good terms with for business purposes. We're just not quite sure how deep those connections go right now, which is why he's still breathing. I called my Reapers tech guy, Glitch, after Marco handed the job over to me, and he's been trying to dig up what he can on Zavier all day.

An unknown player in our territory doesn't usually receive a warm welcome, especially when they neglect to follow protocol and pay the ruling don a healthy percentage of their casino's earnings.

"Okay." Zavier laughs once, but it doesn't reach the eyes still glued to mine. "We can meet in person tomorrow afternoon. I can schedule you in for two." He's trying desperately to control the situation, to gain the power I can see he wants. To everyone else in this room, he might be pulling it off, his domineering alpha attitude is commendable, but that shit doesn't fly with me. There's a miniscule twitch to his left eye as Marco's booming laugh flows through the speaker on the phone.

"You're new here, so I'll allow you this fuck up, but don't do it again. You can deal with J. She speaks for me when it comes to you, Mr. Galanos."

The phone goes dead as Marco hangs up, not wasting time with pleasantries, and now it's my turn to be smug as Zavier places my cell on the huge board table everyone is seated around. His almost-black hair is slicked back, and paired with his clean-shaven jaw that could cut glass and his hazel eyes still boring into mine, I could easily imagine what kind of orgasms this man gives. Shame he's a sly and sneaky bastard, really, but maybe I'll be able to have a little fun at some point. It seems this is going to be an ongoing situation for the Reapers to keep an eye on.

"Tonight is opening night. Would you like me to get someone to show you around, Shadow?" His scoff when he says my name makes me want to slice his balls off, but I remain stoic, calm, not needing to even use words to express that his idea is bullshit.

"I'm here for the meeting." I move to the corner of the room where there are a few spare chairs stacked up and grab one, carrying it back over to the rectangular table. There are eleven men seated at even intervals, Zavier at the head, leaving the opposite end free for me. That was nice of them.

Once I'm sitting down, keeping my back straight so I don't accidentally stab myself with my in-bra dagger, Galanos follows suit and also sits down, tipping his head toward me in some kind of smug acceptance. Not that he had a fucking choice.

"Why are we letting a woman interfere and listen in on this meeting, Mr. Galanos? We are dealing with matters for men. The only use in a casino for a woman that looks like that is to serve our dri—"

I'm out of my chair before the prick in a deep-blue suit sitting to my left finishes speaking and I don't think twice about forcing the ballpoint pen from the table in front of him into his eye socket. It won't kill him if he gets help in time, but he'll definitely be half blind for the rest of his life. Fucker's lucky I didn't just slice his tongue out.

There's a sickening crunchy pop as the pen pierces through his eyeball. Blood squirts out over the table and several of the men move back in shock. Four of them pull their guns and move to aim them in my direction, but not before I've picked up one of the whiskey glasses and thrown it at one of them. It hits him square on the head and knocks him clean out. At the same time, I lift my dress and grab two of my daggers. They fly through the air easily, one of them sticks into a guy's shoulder, forcing him to drop his gun, the other pierces another guy's middle finger, also making him drop his gun. While the knives are flying, so am I, leaping over the table and grabbing another knife from my thigh to hold against the last gun wielder's throat before he can get a shot off.

Yells and shouts echo around the room as more of them move to pull out their weapons—because men like this don't turn up to meetings like this without being armed—and as I lightly scrape my knife over the guy's throat, Zavier yells louder than everyone else.

"Stop! Put your weapons away or I'll kill you all myself." He has a gun in each hand, one pointed in my direction, the other is aimed at the guy beside him. His breathing is short and fast, the anger and control he so desperately tries to keep under wraps is struggling to stay hidden and it's kinda sexy. Especially as he looks over to me, his eyes seeking an explanation.

"He was disrespectful." I shrug, my own breathing still calm as I raise my hands and head back toward my seat.

"You might be the don's bitch, but this is still my turf. Nobody dies in my casino unless I say so." Zavier's words are cutting and I take a mental note of him calling me a bitch, because... just no.

"I don't see any dead bodies, Galanos, so I'm not breaking any rules. Are we going to have this meeting or not? I'm bored and have better things to do than sit in a room full of stuffy men with small dicks." I lean back in my chair and shrug again, hoping they really do just get on with it. Jumping over tables and shit with these heels on wasn't quite as fun as when I'm wearing my boots and I really am looking forward to taking them and this fucking dress off.

Zavier scoffs again, like it's the only thing he's able to do when confronted with someone who doesn't give a shit about his reputation. The other inconsequential men in the room—the uninjured ones—all take their seats while the others lay where they fell until the security dude that led me in here arrives with reinforcements and starts removing them, politely leaving my knives on the table beside Zavier.

"If you're going to insist on being here, please show some respect." As Zavier speaks, the guy in a deep-gray suit near the center of the table looks to me with his snooty nose in the air as if he's just got one over on me. "That goes for *all* of you."

Snooty nose guy sharply turns his head back around to face Zavier, which makes me smile internally, because I won't let these fucks see my emotions.

"Now then, we were discussing the back-room rules and stipulations. Casinos are so new to New York, we need to be careful. If you know of someone who would like an invite, they can go through me first. Understood?"

Various nods and murmurs of agreement flow through the room and I raise a brow, because Galanos is flying close to the knife with this shady bullshit. For Marco to get his cut of this place, we're going to need to keep a close eye on what's going on.

Which I know is gonna fall to me and my Reapers.

I guess I'll be sharpening my poker skills sooner rather than later.

CHAPTER SIX

J

Violence turns me on.

I'm aware that it sounds psychotic, but my life has been a series of fucked up events lined up at the front door of my existence like caffeine addicts at the coffee shop on Monday mornings. It shouldn't surprise me that Galanos's attitude combined with the blood I shed made me wetter than Niagara Falls in the spring.

This explains why a solid hour after leaving the casino, I'm still worked up and craving something that goes beyond my impressive collection of toys. Self-care is important and nothing says "I love me" better than a closet full of vibrators and dildos of all shapes and sizes.

I should be in my bed, enjoying a good night's sleep after an orgasm or two, but as soon as I left the casino, I checked my calls and had a mild panic attack at the sheer number of phone calls with no message from Hallie.

In my world, it means only one thing. She's in trouble. It's a feeling completely foreign to me; the instant rush of anxiety and adrenaline straight to my heart. The number of times I've scoffed at people who make irrational decisions based solely on emotions and here I am, pulling up to my ex-boyfriend's quaint little house in Newark. Or is he my baby-daddy now? Shaking my head to clear it of that errant thought, my eyes scan the neighborhood, the narrow street with family-size cars and tree-lined sidewalks, then I survey the shadows between the rows of homes. They are the typical nineteen-twenties homes that make up the suburban areas of New York and New Jersey. Each one has its own story to tell; immigrant families building their new futures by the sweat of their brows and the will of their hearts. An entire existence before the cookie-cutter homes invaded our states.

The area seems quiet and safe. Porch lights blink in the dead of night as a reminder that fragile lives reside inside.

Except safety is an illusion and quiet is for the deaf. There's no such thing in this world.

Pulling off my helmet, I jump off my bike and rest it on my tank. My brain knows that it's cold as fuck out but my body is pumping with fear, making me sweat beneath my leathers. I've only just met her. I can't lose her now, right? That would make the universe a colossal cunt.

As I cross the street, I tap my thighs to double check that my knives are in place. Before riding out here, I had to take a taxi to my place, change into my gear, and grab my bike. One of my knives got lost in the conference room, probably still stuck in some asshole's hand, so I needed to replace it on my holder.

Once I reach Murphy's front door, I check the lock, cursing at the light screeching of the screen door. A few doors down, a dog barks twice but the quiet quickly returns. There are too many lighted porches here, including Murphy's, so I decide to go in through the back door.

Scaling the wooden fence, I check that nobody is watching before I jump down and slink along the wall until I reach the door. Again with the screen door that sounds like a fucking hyena.

I make a mental note to tell Murph to fix that shit as I pull out the tools I need to pick his lock. Another item to add to the list... get better security around this place. I won't allow my kid to be easily accessible to the monsters of my world.

Quietly, I slink inside, closing the door behind me with just a tiny click of the doorknob. Listening for any signs of struggle, I freeze and concentrate. The back door gives direct access to the kitchen, a *U*-shaped counter with the stove in the middle allows me to crouch behind the breakfast bar. Satisfied with the stillness of it all, I rise just enough to look over the bar and make my way through the kitchen and into the living room with the wooden staircase directly to my right.

There's no way those fuckers aren't going to creak. Dammit.

Before I can place one foot on the first stair, I feel cold hard metal at the back of my head and immediately freeze. My hoodie hides my hair and my face and I'm not sure if this is Murphy protecting our daughter or some random motherfucker thinking he can take what's mine.

I'm on high alert and for the first time in thirteen years, someone else's life is more important than mine, but if I'm dead, then all of this is moot.

"Move and I won't hesitate to blow your fucking head off." I sigh in relief at the familiar sound of Murphy's voice, glad I won't have to organize a cleanup in my daughter's home.

"Shooting someone in the back of the head, huh? Brutal." I chuckle, hoping he'll recognize my voice and the inside joke. Our fathers used to always say that if you must kill, you always look your victim in the eyes.

"Goddammit, J. What the fuck?" The relief in his voice is palpable as he sighs out his words on a long breath. "You got a death wish or something?"

My hands go to my hoodie to pull it down just as I turn around and face my ex.

"Just another Tuesday, I guess." He's not even the first or second person today to point a gun at me. If only he knew how common that is, he'd think twice about exposing Hallie to my universe.

"Christ, you're crazy. What the fuck are you doing here?" The light from the lamppost outside shines directly on him through the window, catching his deep brown eyes as he swings his gaze to the clock. "It's two in the morning."

Ignoring his question for the moment, I sigh and make my way back to the kitchen. "Got any coffee?" Even at sixteen, he was an avid coffee drinker like his dad, much to the exasperation of his mom, who believed drinking coffee so young would stunt his growth.

I'm not short by any standards; at five-seven I'm pretty average, I would say. Murphy has a good five inches on me so it's safe to say his caffeine addiction didn't stunt a damn thing.

"Yeah, I got that fancy shit you used to like. The pods." My gaze follows his every move as I sit on the stool at the breakfast bar. First, he closes the door, then he turns on the light. I'm guessing he's trying to keep from waking up Hallie. It is a school night, after all. "Hallie gets on me that it's environmentally stupid—her words—to use pods, but I refuse to give up my coffee."

I can't help the curve at the corners of my mouth. I like predictable and his habits still being true today have a weird warmth spreading in my chest.

"She called me a dozen times tonight without leaving a message. I thought she was in danger." Murphy stills for a second, like the idea of her being in danger physically affects him, before he sighs, a quiet chuckle escaping him as he reaches for the open metal safe and puts his gun away.

"She's thirteen. Everything is urgent and drama is her lifeline." Facing me, he grins. "You'll get used to it. To be honest, I'm still adjusting to her mood swings. One second I'm the love of her life and the next I'm the cause of all her troubles."

I shrug, my memories from my teenage years a distant echo because I chose to put it all in a steel drawer.

"I need to have a conversation with her about boundaries and late-night phone calls. It takes me almost an hour to get here, I won't be summoned."

Murphy chuckles again, a mocking edge to his amusement that gets under my skin more than I'd like to admit.

"You'll get used to it," is all he says.

"No, that's the whole point. I don't have time to get used to it, Murph. I have a job and responsibilities so I can't be at her beck and call. She needs to learn." Teenagers can't be any worse than some of my younger Reapers. Discipline and order are the best path to obedience.

"I'll get right on that." His amusement morphs into something edgier, more frustrated. Sarcasm.

My spine straightens and my eyes narrow. "Why are you getting pissy all of a sudden?" I don't do subtle, it's not in my genes.

The machine rumbling as a thin line of dark coffee falls into an espresso cup gives us a minute to step back from our growing little spat. By the time the cup is full and the machine is quiet, Murphy's features are more relaxed. More than mine, at least.

"I'll talk to her, Jaybear, but just a heads up... she's a lot like you so it's not always easy." His raised brow is a challenge. He wants me to contradict him but I can't. I'm not easy, never have been, and I'm even worse now. I like that she's like me, it means she's got the heart of a survivor.

"You don't have to talk to her, I can do it. Can't be that hard." I mumble that last part because, fucking hell, she's barely thirteen and living a quiet, sheltered life. I've dealt with various monsters and killers on a daily basis, this will be a piece of cake.

"Always so cocky, huh? You've known her all of five minutes and all of a sudden you're better at this than me?" Mechanically, he hands me my coffee with a spoon even though I take it black. My smile is instant and genuine, feeling almost foreign on my lips. I'd forgotten how it felt to have someone know me, someone know that I like to stir my coffee while it cools down even if there's nothing there to stir together. No one else knows anything beyond me killing and cleaning up the messes. This feels more intimate than actual sex, to be honest. I'm The Shadow for a reason and, until this very second, I basked in the comfort of being invisible to most.

"Here you go, black like a starry night." It's like thirteen years was just a hot minute as his words reach out and remind me why I fell in love with him so quickly back then.

"Thank you." I can be polite.

"You're welcome." Watching him fill a cup of whole milk and put it into the microwave stirs up a whole other set of emotions. Memories of us as kids, so fucking in love, staying up late despite our parents' best efforts to keep us apart on school nights, rush to the forefront of my mind and that fucking heat in my chest grows hot enough to give me heartburn.

"I need to know something, Jaybear." My walls come crashing down, my senses on high alert. Nothing good ever comes from those words put together in that way.

"I may not be able to answer, Murph, and you need to be okay with that." Bringing the hot mug to my lips, I keep my eyes fixed on him over the rim. Not only can I not tell him about anything related to the Mancinis', but I don't want to. I refuse to place him in the line of fire.

"I gathered from your stealthy entrance that you're not working some office job from nine to five." His sarcasm doesn't sit well with me but I can't deny the truth behind his words.

Still, I scoff, shaking my head as I put the mug back on the counter. "You taught me how to pick a lock, Murph. Hypocrite much?"

"We were twelve, it was exciting."

"I was a child and you corrupted me." I can barely keep a straight face at my accusation. Back then, I followed my father everywhere he went. If a boy could do it, I could do it, and my dad was completely on board with that line of thought.

"Right. So the time you showed me how to hotwire a car, that was my fault?"

I shrug at his words like he's hit the nail on the head.

Murphy leans on the counter, his elbows and forearms pressed against the faux marble as his face leans dangerously close. He was my north star, the boy who respected me above anyone else. Well, besides his father, that is. That man hung the moon.

So, it's no surprise the effect his proximity has on me. The scent of mint with a hint of engine oil from his hours working on cars and motorcycles. It stirs up memories I can't allow myself to linger on.

"I can't believe it's really you." The microwave beeps but he doesn't move.

"Don't." I'm not stupid, I know how to read a room.

"Don't what, Jaybear?" Is he inching closer or is that me leaning into him?

"Don't read more into this than there really is." The chemistry we shared from back when hormones controlled our bodies is back and refuses to be ignored. It's in the crackle of electricity bouncing from his exposed skin to mine.

"I'm not reading anything, just waiting on my warm milk." Those chocolate brown eyes that used to reel me in every fucking time are boring into me like some kind of magic spell, keeping me from looking away.

I don't answer because his breath is suddenly close enough for me to taste on the tip of my tongue as it darts out to lick my suddenly dry lips.

"I didn't think you could get more beautiful." He reaches out with one finger, pushing a strand of my blonde hair back behind my ear. "Yet here you are, fucking stunning."

My eyes dart to the door as my heart hammers behind my ribcage. This leather is keeping all the heat inside and I can't even blame my coffee since I've only taken a sip. It's him. His presence, his scent, the way his eyes see only me. I haven't had that kind of undivided attention since I was fifteen and having sex for the first time with the boy I loved more than life itself.

"You're half asleep and talking out of your ass, Murph." I order my body to get up and off this stool but I'm held down by the mere force of his stare.

"Fucking. Stunning." He repeats the words like I didn't hear him the first time.

I'm not blind and I don't lack any self-confidence, but listening to others give me compliments makes me uncomfortable. What am I supposed to say? Thank you? Why would I thank someone for commenting on my looks? So, I deflect. It's what I do.

"You're full of shit." His lips are close enough that if I dart my tongue out again, I'll touch him.

"Stay tonight. Have breakfast with us tomorrow." I blink, the spell he has on me dissipating just a little.

"I can't..." I don't know why I can't but it feels like the right answer.

"You can't or you won't?"

Fuck, when did he become so mature? Well, yeah... probably in the last thirteen years while he was raising our daughter. Alone.

"Tell me about her." I change the subject to give myself some time.

There's a pause, an intense moment where our eyes communicate in silence.

"Do you remember when your mom got so scared from your fall out of the tree house?"

The memory assaults me like a fucking semi going top speed. I didn't break anything but I had a big bruise along the outside of my thigh and a sprained ankle. My mother held me in her arms for two days, refusing to leave my side, afraid I'd "do something stupid and be taken away".

"Yeah, what about it?" My voice sounds bored but inside I'm shaking with how much I miss my parents on a visceral level.

"That's how I feel every fucking day, Jordyn. Every time she goes to school, I'm afraid she'll get kidnapped. Every time she's at soccer practice, I'm afraid she'll break a leg. Every time she rides her bike, I'm afraid she'll get hit by a car. If she sneezes, I think she has some incurable disease. But then she'll smile at me and I can't imagine this world without her, or she'll giggle, or hug me just a little bit longer than usual and I can't breathe from the love I have for her. She's... everything. She's my whole fucking world." I stare at this man he's become, the father I knew he would be, and regret swallows me up like that fucking whale from the Pinocchio movie.

"You just told me more about you than about her." I point out the obvious because the feelings swimming inside me are too raw to examine and acknowledge.

"Well, stay for breakfast and get to know her."

That sneaky bastard. Well played.

Before I even know what's happening, he leans in and with the slightest touch of his lips against mine, he whispers, "My pancakes are the best in the tristate area."

"I'll be the judge of that."

CHAPTER SEVEN

J

The tension between Murphy and me is just one reason I declined his invitation to get a few hours of shut-eye beside him in bed. It's not that I don't want to, because holy shit he's grown into any woman's wet dream, but there's no way I'd have been able to lie in bed with my ex-boyfriend while I was horny as fuck without, well, fucking. I don't want to completely screw up the whole parent thing before I've even had a chance to get started.

I say *completely*... I'm a woman with needs and Murphy's, well, Murphy.

The little early morning phone call after he'd gone to bed may just have been my downfall, but there I was, wrapped up in the blankets Murphy brought downstairs for me so I could sleep on the couch, with my phone in my hand and a throbbing need in my pussy. What was a woman to do?

So I called him. He answered within one ring, his deep, rumbling voice like a caress with one sentence.

"What do you need, Jaybear?"

"You." I barely recognized myself.

His guttural groan described all the things he wanted to do with that word. "Fuck. Come upstairs."

"I can't. We can't." I wanted to punch myself in the face for being such a fucking confusing dick.

"Then I'm coming down." The sound of his bed sheets rustling sent a thrill straight to my clit, imagining all the things he would do to me once he got me in bed again. But I was trying so hard to be this sensible person, not rushing into the situation.

"No, Murph. But fuck, I'm so wet." I couldn't help it. The words just spewed outta my mouth.

"J, you're killing me, here."

"Are you hard?"

"As a fucking rock." His tone was darker, huskier, like he was feeling exactly the same as me.

Uncontrollable.

"Touch yourself. Let me hear how wet you are for me, gorgeous."

Even at that moment, he was willing to give me everything I needed.

I slipped my hand beneath my panties and pushed a finger into my pussy, spreading my wetness around before taking it out and sucking on it, loudly, so he could hear every slurp.

"Like that?"

"Exactly like that." His breaths were becoming shorter pants, which turned me the fuck on even more imagining how he was pumping himself.

Pushing my fingers back into my pussy, then out, rubbing at my clit, I moved faster, moaning loud enough for him to hear everything through the phone. "Fuck, Murph."

"Put your phone on speaker and place it on your stomach, then play with your nipple at the same time." Sexy instructions are a weakness for me. I crave it, even, and immediately complied.

"How wet are you?" His whispered words sounded even hotter through the loudspeaker, like he was straining to contain himself.

"Like you've just pumped your load inside me."

The call consisted of a lot of heavy breaths, grunts, moans, so many *fucks* and *yeses,* until we both came hard and fast, leaving me wishing I was ready to just go head first into this with him. Ready to go and climb into his bed and do this thing for real.

I sigh at the memory, knowing it wasn't exactly my best decision. I seem to be doing that a lot lately.

"Mom?"

That one word is like an arrow shooting straight through my stomach and almost knocking me on my ass, completely ruining my daydream from the early hours of this morning. But I'm not mad. How could I be?

When I thought I'd lost her, hearing someone call me by that name became an impossibility, but now? Now it's my reality, and a lump forms in my throat as I try to reply from my couch-haven of blankets. Instead, I turn, facing the beautiful young woman I helped create, throwing her a wink, and gesture for her to come and join me.

"Morning, Kid." It's barely dawn, and apparently she hasn't hit the sleeping-until-lunchtime phase of teenage-dom. The curtains are drawn, but there's a dim light from the TV I wasn't really watching.

"Are you taking me to school today? I usually take the bus, but it'd really annoy Bridget if I arrive on the back of your bike. She told me I was lying when I said my mom rode a motorcycle." Hallie sits down next to me as if this were all completely natural, burying herself under the blanket to get comfortable. "Though, to be fair, everyone did think my mom was dead until I posted about it on social media."

That statement puts another lump in my throat that I'm choosing to ignore as I listen to my daughter tell me about her friends and frenemies—Bridget being one of them—all of her own accord. I didn't have to ask any questions. She's just opening up to me and putting all her trust in me and it's something I've never experienced with such ease before.

It's fucking terrifying and amazing all at the same time.

I may have to find out who this Bridget is and... no, she's a thirteen-year-old girl. This protective streak is a little outrageous.

"Ah, both my girls together. I could get used to this. Coffee?" Murphy's sleep-laden voice pierces my senses as Hallie and I turn to see him leaning against the door jamb.

"Please."

"Orange juice for me, please, Dad."

We respond at the same time, laughing when Murphy rolls his head dramatically and faux-curtseys like our own personal maid.

When he returns from the kitchen, Hallie and I both groan in appreciation for the drinks he hands over, each taking a sip. Her little giggle as I wink down at her snuggled next to me is enough to make a grown man cry from happiness. It's so fucking pure...

I know that them believing I was still dead would have been a lot safer for them, but fuck me, that giggle. This kid. *My* kid. She's fucking magical.

Murphy looks over his own coffee mug toward us from his position in the armchair, his ankles crossed on the rug in front of him. His eyes tell a whole myriad of stories, remind me of a million different things from my past, and promise a whole lot of something for my future. A future I'm trying desperately to keep safe for these two right here.

The how, I'm not exactly sure of yet, but the why... because they've been through enough, they have each other, they have love, they have everything they could possibly want and need. And I know bringing me into this beautiful picture is going to fuck shit up.

This perfect little morning is something I think I'll treasure forever though. I'm not much of a hugger but this kid is impossible to ignore.

"Mom's taking me to school on her bike."

Murphy's eyes falter at her use of the word mom—must be strange to hear it from her after so long—but he quickly regains his composure as he realizes what she just spurted out before downing the rest of her juice and jumping up from the couch.

He begins laughing as she makes her way to the door for the hall. "Not a chance, little lady. Bus will be here in twenty minutes. Good try."

"But Daaa—"

"End of discussion, Peanut. Go get ready for school."

The tone he uses is authoritative, completely unlike the boy I once knew... I like it. It sends a tingle between my legs, making me crave him again as much as I did last night. But it's still a bad idea.

Totally a bad idea.

"I'll follow behind the bus on my bike. Apparently, Bridget called her a liar so she has something to prove. Not that she should have to, but I'm all for showing up smug bitches in front of her friends." I sip at the last dregs of my coffee, a little sad that it's gone and wishing I could have another before I head out. Coffee made by someone else always tastes better.

"You don't have to. Bridget will be her best friend again by next week. They've been on and off like lovers since kindergarten." Murphy stands and holds out his hand for my empty mug. "I'll make us another." It's not a question, he's just going to do it, and there's something hot as fuck about him anticipating my needs like that.

"Thanks." I stand and follow him through to the kitchen to continue our conversation. "I know I don't have to go, but I want to. I'm not working until later, so I've got plenty of time."

"You gonna tell me what you're up to these days, Jay-bear?" Pouring the coffee, he raises a questioning brow as he looks at me, but he knows I'm not about to give him a straight answer.

"No." I take the fresh mug of coffee he offers, shrugging as I blow the hot liquid over the rim.

"Ca—"

"No, you can't ask questions. And yes, I'll keep my work away from Hallie. That's all you need to know." My interruption has Murphy taking a deep, steadying breath, and I know he wants more answers than I'm willing to give, but I just can't.

"Ready! Bus is outside. See ya later, Dad." Hallie bounds into the kitchen to hug her dad, kissing his cheek before turning to me. "Will you still be here after school?"

Her little eyes are so wide and round and pleading, and I now realize why some parents find it so hard to leave their kids for a weekend away.

"Sorry, Kid. Gotta work. But I'll be by again soon, and I'm following you to school so we can show Bridget that you're not a liar." I wink at her, placing my mug down and heading to the front door where my leather jacket is hanging on the hook. I didn't get undressed, so I'm still in my riding clothes from the early hours of this morning. I'll head back to my place and shower before checking in with my Reapers this afternoon.

"What? Seriously? Yaaas! She's going to eat shit!"

"Hallie!" Murphy scolds her, but he has a smirk on his face he's trying desperately to hide. Mine... not so hidden. I can't help the laugh that escapes.

"Sorry, Dad." She looks suitably chastised as she bats her lashes at him and I smile again at her relationship with her dad. She has him wrapped around her little finger and he loves it. And they're both happy. "Anyway, laters, Dad!"

She bounds out the front door, school bag in hand, and heads toward the yellow bus sitting on the corner with a few other kids boarding. Before she climbs on, she looks over to me watching her, waves her little hand, grinning widely, and shouts, "Later, Mom!"

Fucking kid's gonna be the death of me.

"You sure you want to show up at a school full of kids just to prove our daughter isn't a liar?" This is also something he already knows the answer to.

"Abso-fucking-lutely."

He smirks, that beautiful fucking smirk that makes my knees weak, and it's then I realize how close we're standing to each other in the open entrance to his home. His scent overrides anything else, his warmth causes my hairs to stand on end just to be near him, and his every breath is like an invitation to kiss his plump lips. I'm leaning back against the door jamb, my palms on the frame behind me, and he leans forward, one hand resting above my head, the other coming in to stroke my chin with his thumb. He's intoxicating.

Before I can speak, his mouth is on mine in the most gentle kiss known to man. We don't move, we just stay there for a few moments, breathing each other in with our joined lips until the honk of the school bus as it drives off catches our attention and I take a deep breath as he pulls away.

"I should go. Made a promise and all that." I nod, patting Murphy's arm like a fucking dick as I walk away, not hanging around to hear or do anything else with this temptation of a man.

I slide my helmet on over my head and straddle my bike, starting the engine and loving the rumble, the smell, the sheer sense of power between my thighs as I roll back the throttle and easily catch up to the school bus.

The school isn't far away, so it doesn't take long before the bus pulls up to let the kids off and I ride over close to the entrance to wait. I don't remove my helmet as I'm scanning the area; the people who killed my family still want me dead, and when they all thought I was... Hallie and Murphy were safe.

Fuck.

Maybe this isn't such a good idea after all. I've been brash and rushed head first into this situation, using fucking none of the actual skills I've learned over the years that have kept me alive so far.

Hallie comes rushing over at the same time I see another face from my past, but it's too late to send my kid away and pretend I'm not here for her.

They look over curiously at Hallie wrapping her arms around me and I awkwardly pat her back before moving away, ready to ride the hell on out of here.

I need to get to my Reapers, and I need to get my fucking head screwed on straight, because this little dalliance into parenthood may just be one of my biggest fuck-ups in a long time.

CHAPTER EIGHT

J

"Wussup, Boss?" Shoo pipes up from the kitchen where he's making milkshakes for the crew, barely looking my way when I walk into our clubhouse. His big paws could kill bears, if ever we were attacked by one in the middle of Brooklyn, and yet here he is making the Reapers happy with his ice-cream delight.

"We've got a job." The entire lot of them groan at my news. Not because they're upset about cleaning up some guy's guts spread all over his kitchen floor, but because those milkshakes are definitely going to waste tonight. "Shoo, Tab, you're coming with me. So suit up, it's a messy one."

With an "On it, Boss" reply and a grunt or two, they get up from their spots and head to their quarters. It's Fizz and Binx's night off, and the shaven-headed pocket rocket of our crew, Flower, is on another job with Crank, our main mechanical man. As I wait for Shoo and Tab to get their shit, I put away some of the trash and empty glasses they've left out, mainly out of boredom. We got this house after a job some years ago, when the owner lost his head because he'd gotten himself mixed up with the wrong people.

Literally. It was severed from his body, dumped into a vat of concrete, and thrown into the Hudson. His body was cremated alongside the wood from a house we demolished because of an infestation of rats. Sad, really. The house was nice. Vince Borelli? Not so much. He threatened Marco Mancini's wife at her place of business. Needless to say, that was the last bad decision he ever made. With him gone and no next of kin to worry about, we took over his five-bedroom house his late mother left him and made it into our headquarters.

Although, most days, it's just a man cave with the lingering smell of unchecked testosterone.

"Hey, Boss, we takin' the van or the truck?" Closing the dishwasher, I glance at Tab, who's always no nonsense and ready to get shit done and done right. He's a big boy, his head an inch shy of touching the top of the doorway.

"The van. I have a feeling we're gonna need a shit load of products. Apparently, The Butcher had an ax to grind. Or... a knife to whet?" I shrug then jump at the sound of Shoo belting out a laugh from across the room.

"Holy shit, Boss, did you just make a joke?" Rolling my eyes, I don't bother answering. Half the time these guys think I lost my heart on the wrong side of the GW Bridge when I first crossed over from New Jersey. Little do they know that, as of late, that heart has been working overtime and it's all Hallie Gallagher's fault.

"Shut the fuck up. Let's go."

These guys are like my family and we bust each other's chops like we're a brotherhood, but I have to hide my smirk and be the boss they respect or else they'll be lost little lambs, and nobody wants to see three-hundred-pound lambs razing the city, completely out of control.

Tab and I ride our bikes, one ahead of the van, the other far enough behind that it doesn't raise any suspicions from the law. It's late and it's cold but we've got a job that's best done in the middle of the night when the naïve population sleeps, certain that evil like us doesn't exist.

We don't kill the guys... we just clean up the mess. Well, okay, to be completely honest, sometimes I do kill the guys as well, but that's different.

The van takes a left but I keep going, continuing another two streets down before making my turn. I know where they're going and if I have eyes on me, it won't look like I'm following the guys. At midnight, Brooklyn is still alive in certain corners, completely asleep in others. A few errant teens whistle as I pass by, admiring my bike, but my mind is too lost in thoughts of Murphy and that kiss he gave me when I left this morning. How is he not pissed off at me? If the tables were turned, I think I'd be livid. Hell, he'd be fucking dead if I'd thought he'd abandoned our daughter to save his own ass. Just thinking about it makes me grip my handle bars with more force than necessary.

Yet, here he is. Accepting that I'm back in his life after being forced to raise our girl by himself. Either he's a fucking saint or...

No. I can't think like that. I cannot constantly decide that everyone has an ulterior motive or a reason to kill me. There's no fucking way. I know how to read people and Murph loves Hallie more than anything else in the world and hurting me would hurt her.

Saint it is, then.

I suppose opposites attract. Isn't that what we're always told? My devilish red to his angelic white? Maybe that was why it was so fucking hard to leave him this morning, the urge to push him back inside the house and sit on his face to see if his eating skills had improved was strong. After all, I was the first pussy he'd ever tasted, and even back then he had quite the talented tongue. I bet he could...

A horn blares through the quiet of the night and right away I realize we've crossed over the Brooklyn Bridge and into Manhattan. I flip off the asshole who thinks he owns the fucking street just because his car has a German name, forcing myself not to cut him off and show him my knife collection up close and personal.

I swear, these Lower Manhattan fuckers need to be leashed and whipped into submission.

It takes me another ten minutes to get to our job site. I park behind the building; the alley is as dark as can be expected with a brick wall cutting off access just a few feet away. Pocketing the keys, I take off my helmet and let my gaze follow the straight lines of the brick patterns all around the narrow space. The buildings are about five stories high with only a couple of lights still on, one flashing in rhythm with whatever television show the tenant is watching. In the distance, a dog barks twice, which is the only sound that disturbs the constant humming of the city that never sleeps.

My baby will be fine. Time to get to work.

We've all walked in at different times, wearing nondescript clothing just in case we run into anyone. My cover story is something about a boyfriend upstairs. The key is to be vague and if the person asks more questions, just push on through with a "nunya business, lady." Experience taught me that those who usually ask questions are women over the age of eighty. I hate to offend my elders but a girl's gotta do her job.

When I get to the apartment, I check around to make sure no one's watching. Shoo put a black sticker on the peephole across the hall, just in case, but I'd done my research before going to the clubhouse. The guy across the hall was just taken to a medical residence due to his age and progressing cancer. Still, the sticker is reassuring.

By the time I'm inside, the guys are all suited up in black rubber and face masks with their hair in full-on hair nets to avoid getting any DNA in the apartment. As of right now, no one knows this guy's dead. Marco called me with minimal information. Devon Quinn, Marco's brother-in-law—or one of three, I guess—was sending a message all the way across the fucking pond to his enemies trying to off him in the New World.

Idiots.

"Looks like The Butcher went all Jackson Pollock on this guy." We all stop and, like a slow-motion movie, turn to Shoo with matching furrowed brows. It takes him a second to realize we're not moving before he shrugs like it's no big deal. "What? I watch documentaries in my down time and I happen to appreciate good art. Sue me." His thick Brooklyn accent only makes this whole fucking conversation more surreal. "I like to think I'm a cultivated thug."

If we weren't in the middle of a job where silence is key, Tab and I would be outright laughing. Fizz is going to be disappointed she missed this.

That said, he's right. Devon went fucking psycho on this guy. His face is sliced from one side to the other like a pumpkin on Halloween. Trick or treat, indeed. Judging from the various pools of blood, he chopped off one limb after the other; his goal was pain more than anything else. Or maybe he was trying to get information out of him. In any case, our job is cleaning up, not solving the crime by figuring out the motive. Although, after all these years, I'd probably make a great detective. If I survived long enough outside the mob. Which I wouldn't. Nobody leaves the family alive.

Nobody.

Even Enzo, Marco's most trusted man and one of his brothers-in-law, had to find a way to stay on the job or else disappear forever. It's the way it is. You know when you step inside that the only way out is in a body bag... if you're lucky. Most likely, you end up like this guy, right here.

It takes us the better part of three hours to clean this modern art off the fucking walls. The next time I'm at Devon's gym, I'll make sure to thank him for the work. With my fist in his pretty-boy British face.

"Fucking Christ, there's a drop up in the corner over there." My eyes follow Tab's finger and no shit... there's a splash of red in the far corner of the room.

"Get the black light out, let's make sure we're thorough. Guy's got a sister so she'll be coming around looking for him at some point. We don't want the cops sniffing around and finding cause to make it a crime scene." No body, no evidence, no cause for an investigation.

The vibration in my back pocket gets my attention. Only bad news comes around at three in the morning.

Murphy's name flashes on the screen and my heart goes into overdrive. It's not even romantic, it's fear. Outright, soul-crushing fear like I've never felt before... not since the night my parents were gunned down in cold blood.

Hallie.

"Is she all right?" I don't bother with pleasantries or a ridiculous "hello" like I don't know who it is.

"Calm down, tiger. She's fine. Been asleep for the last six hours."

I frown. *What the fuck?*

"I'm the one who can't sleep."

Aren't there teas for that?

"So you thought calling me would be the equivalent of a sleeping pill?" His deep, dark chuckle does things to me.

"No, Jaybear, I figured you'd be the only person I know to still be awake." This makes me pause and think about the situation. Murph isn't stupid, he knows I'm not out here helping the elderly cross the street. But if he ever found out I'm working for the Mancini family, he might not be able to forgive me for that. The Irish mob and the Italian mafia don't even remotely get along. Their truce is hanging on by the thread of their ball sacks and finding out I'm not only still alive but in the deep end of the Mancini family? It would only mean one thing... war.

Murphy would kill me himself before bringing death to his front door.

More reason for me to keep my distance from them. It's the only way to make sure they're safe.

"You good, J?" Tab's deep voice is so close I nearly jump at the sound but I don't miss the heavy intake of Murphy's breath.

"You're busy, then. I'll let you go." He hangs up and I'm left here, completely at a loss.

Well, fuck.

CHAPTER NINE
MURPHY

That was a dick move.

I knew I was being an asshole as I hung up the phone but, for some reason, I couldn't stop myself from doing it. The green-eyed monster took over my brain and all I could see was J with some burly sounding guy, doing whatever it was they were doing. For all I know, he was her mechanic asking her if everything was going okay with her bike.

Dammit, what is she doing to me?

Looking at my clock on my phone, I realize sleep isn't going to happen. Being productive by starting on work now would *maybe* allow me to leave the garage earlier tomorrow. One can hope.

Firing up the laptop, I click on my spreadsheets and line them up on different tabs. Each tab holds a different list of vehicles with matching plates. Then, going into the system, I search out numbers that are available and give those numbers to cars we're reselling. I know it's not exactly legal but my name is nowhere to be seen on any of the papers and no names are registered to any of the cars. Even if anyone were to have doubts about our operation, every paper and computer trail would lead to a dead end. We made sure of it.

It's not until after twenty minutes of work that I wonder if I could find J's plate number on this system and from there, surely the DMV would have her address. Once the thought takes root, I can't stop my fingers from roaming the system until I get a hit.

Like a teenager who's just found a handwritten note from the girl he likes sitting in his locker, I'm acutely aware of the butterflies doing some kind of dance in my guts. What I'm doing is stalkerish and a bit douchebaggy but my curiosity is slowly killing me.

Also, there's Hallie and I have to keep her safe. At least, that's what I tell myself.

The address that flashes on my screen is located on West Eleventh, which, at this time of night, shouldn't be more than a twenty-minute ride, probably less. My gaze flicks to the side as though I can see through the walls that Hallie is fast asleep.

I could do this. She's thirteen, she can stay alone for less than an hour. Hell, she probably won't ever know that I left the house.

Jumping out of the chair before I can talk myself out of it, I pull on a sweatshirt and grab my boots before scratching a few words on a piece of paper that I place on the fridge downstairs. If Hallie wakes up, it'll be because she's thirsty, and with any luck, she won't be sleepwalking and will know that I've stepped out for a bit. In any case, she can call me if she really needs me.

Locking up, I run to the truck and blow hot air into my hands. Fuck, I should have brought gloves, this cold is like nails being planted in my skin. With one last look at Hallie's darkened room upstairs, I put the truck in reverse and head somewhere between the financial district and midtown.

I'm completely lost in thought the entire ride over, wondering why I'm driving in the middle of the night to an address I don't know to see if the girl that got away thirteen years ago is fucking some random guy.

Fucking hell, I think I'm losing my mind and she's the one who's hidden it somewhere close to her heart. I hope.

Fifteen minutes later, I'm pulling up along the curb to... nothing but closed shops with apartments upstairs. If she's home, her bike is obviously in a private underground parking garage because it's not in the street. Also, who the fuck rides a motorcycle in the dead of winter?

My girl, apparently.

I'm not sure what I expected to see. Had I really thought she'd be hanging out on the sidewalk randomly hoping I'd drive up and park? What a fucking idiot. But then again, I've always made ridiculous decisions when it came to her.

I can't remember a single day when I didn't love Jordyn O'Neill and I don't think that will ever change. It's why I always came back to the diner after she'd "disappeared". It's where we had our burgers as teens. Our first date, our first kiss. About the only first that place doesn't hold is the first time I told her I loved her. That was when we made love for the first time. It's cheesy but then we were fifteen and love was the easiest thing to celebrate.

Fuck this.

Snatching up my phone from the holder in the car, I search out J's name and press call before I chicken out.

"Still can't sleep?" She answers on the first ring and her throaty voice takes me by surprise.

"I'm at your place." I look up to see if any new lights have turned on but that's ridiculous with the number of floors there are.

"Are you now?" She doesn't sound convinced or even surprised, like the idea of me finding her apartment is too inconceivable.

"Yeah, I've got my ways." Her laughter ringing on the other side of the line goes straight to my dick. It's such a rare, pure even, sound that I want to bask in it for hours. Then it hits me. "Do you live on top of some restaurant that serves sushi?" I know the answer before she even replies but hope springs eternal and all that shit.

"Sorry, no restaurants anywhere in sight from my window." She sounds amused and that, at least, makes me happy because anything that makes her smile is pure happiness for me.

"So, tell me, Murph. What made you get in your truck at..." She pauses like she's checking her phone or watch or whatever, then continues. "Four thirty in the morning?"

The answer is so simple that it just rolls off the tongue. "You."

"Me, huh?"

"Yeah, Jaybear. I just..." Fuck, I'm such an idiot. "I lost you once and the thought that this... *us* is all in my head is doing me in." I can hear her releasing a heavy breath on the other side of the line but I don't push, I just let her take her time.

"I have a job, Murph. And sometimes that job means I'm surrounded by men. It has nothing to do with us... it's just my job." All I actually hear is, *blah blah blah, surrounded by men,* so I try to erase the mental image that goes along with those words. "And Murphy?" Hope springs all over again. "I don't know if there's an us but I'm trying really hard to stay away because..." She pauses again, her breathing coming in and out a lot faster, like she's trying to fight some kind of urge to share her emotions.

"Just tell me, J, I can handle it." I don't think I can but I'll fake it until I make it.

"I'm no good for you, Murph, and I'm definitely no good for Hallie." Her words are whispered like she's ashamed or she doesn't want the universe to hear her admission.

"Let us be the judge of that. And in any case, you don't really have a choice, do you? Whether you like it or not, you're her mother and she wants to get to know you." We're silent again and I'm starting to freeze my ass off, parked out here in the February winter with the truck turned off.

"Go home, Murphy. I'll call you."

"All right, Jaybear." She hangs up and a part of me is lost to her forever... sitting right next to her heart for the rest of time.

When I turn over the engine, I take one last glance up at the building and wish I could see her watching me from above, but that's just the dream of a teenage boy from thirteen years ago, waiting for the mother of his child to come back home.

CHAPTER TEN

J

The cameras seem to follow me wherever I go inside this casino, and I make sure to find ways to keep my middle finger visible to whoever's watching without outrightly waving it around. I know I'm not the only one they're following but I do love to be defiant when the opportunity arises.

The tech systems here all seem pretty high standard. From the mics and earpieces on the croupiers, the cameras dotted around the huge space, and the two rounds of security to get inside, it's a lot more than I've seen in the casino on the other side of the city.

From the research my own tech guy, Glitch, gathered, Zavier's tech guy is a bit of an unknown, which is annoying as fuck. Glitch can find anything on anyone, and we have all we need on the rest of Zavier's "employees", but it seems this one is gonna take some more digging. Whoever it is, they seem to know what they're doing.

"All in!" The tall, thin man in a dusty gray suit sitting at the poker table with me pushes his remaining poker chips into the center of the table with a smug grin in my direction.

We started the game with seven of us and I've gradually taken all their chips, leaving just the two of us. Going all in may sound like the move of a big boy who's positive of a win, but calling him makes barely a dent in my own pile of chips. I'm also positive he's been cheating, and the croupier is in on it. The fact that Zavier's amazing tech guy hasn't been able to pick up on it is just one reason they should've done this properly and included Marco. We have ways of vetting potential employees that would guarantee this wouldn't happen.

"Call." I casually push my own chips into the center of the table, giving absolutely fuck all away with my face.

There are still two cards left to come out, the turn and the river, but whatever they are, he won't beat the straight flush I already have. The croupier deals the last two cards, revealing the three of clubs and the ace of spades. I remain still, motionless, because no more betting can be done—he has nothing left to bet with. It's all down to these last cards in play.

"Ha. Four of a kind. Aces." The cheating fuck lowers his cards, face-up, showing two aces, and the croupier is about to push the chips over to the thin man without even waiting to see what I have—he's that sure he dealt this man the winning hand. Little does he know, in a casino like this, I never lose.

"Royal flush. Hearts."

The croupier has trouble hiding his surprise and immediately pushes the chips in my direction instead of to the thin guy. Thin Guy, on the other hand, looks at me with disgust clear in his eyes as he stands from his stool.

"You cheated." He points at me. I fucking hate it when people point at me. I don't know what it is, it just irritates the shit out of me. Of course, I don't let him see that.

"How so?" I tilt my head to the side and bat my lashes at him as I stack my chips in front of me.

This evening didn't require me to be in a dress, thank fuck, but I've got to admit the black pants and white, wide-collared, button-up shirt I'm wearing do give off sexy vibes. Paired with my low-heeled boots, perfect for riding my baby, and some black kohl around my eyes, I've at least tried to fit in a little around here. That was part of the agreement Zavier and I came to. Marco could have his hand in this casino to a small extent, and I'd be allowed access to check in on things if I didn't dress like a "biker bum".

I almost punched him right in the throat when he came up with that idea in our meeting last week.

Marco isn't one for making ridiculous deals like this with people, makes them feel like they have more power than they really do, but Marco wants a connection that Zavier has, so we're in the business of keeping him happy. For now.

"You shouldn't even be in here. This place is for men or whores. You're neither. Unless you're gonna come ride my dick while you give me my chips back." Thin Guy moves toward me, standing directly in front of me. I remain sitting on the tall black-and-gold stool, glaring up at him, readying a poker chip to jam in this dude's eye socket.

"I think you'll find the lady won, Mr. Wright." A warmth spreads across my neck and I know exactly who has just approached, slowly placing his hand on my shoulder. It isn't for comfort; this is his way of telling me to stay seated and not kill the fucker in front of me.

"She cheated, Mr. Gallanos. Surely, she should be removed from the premises. This is outrageous." Thin guy is spitting mad, and I almost laugh, but I'm currently concentrating on not breaking Zavier's wrist for touching me.

"You know what they say about sore losers?" My index finger and thumb are barely an inch apart as an answer to my own question and I swear the guy is going to spontaneously combust right here. Small dick syndrome can be a touchy subject for men like this.

Zavier's grip on my shoulder tightens, and oh no he fucking didn't...

"What she means, Mr. Wright, is good game, well played—"

"No it fucking isn't." I turn to smirk at Zavier, and his hazel eyes bore into mine almost erotically. There's a tension there, a seriousness that he wants me to pay attention to, and I know how to read a room. I take a deep breath, deciding this isn't a battle I want to pick, and plaster on a sickly-sweet smile. "Good game, Mr. Wright. Well played."

"Now hang o—"

One of the security guys appears almost from nowhere and begins leading Mr. Wright away. His protests are quickly cut off as he looks at the giant beast of a man showing him the way out. The croupier remains silent the whole time, presumably organizing a new deck for the next round of poker starting up in an hour.

"Get your fucking hand off me." I speak under my breath, my teeth gritted, but I know Zavier can hear me because he chuckles and removes said hand.

"Always so feisty, Shadow. Are you like that in the bedroom?" He fake shudders. "Ooh, I hope you are." He leans down to sniff my exposed neck. With my hair slicked back into a single french braid, he has easy access.

I roll my eyes and discreetly grab his dick behind me, keeping my eyes straight forward as I say my next words. "You'll never find out, Gallanos. Step. The fuck. Back."

His chuckle fills my eardrum and he pretends to bite my lobe, but he does step back and I loosen my grip on his now-hard dick, eventually letting go—it would have been a waste not to feel the whole thing.

"Would you care to join me in my office, Shadow?" Zavier holds a hand out to me to help me stand. "Carlos, can you take Ms. Shadow's chips to the cage cashier and have them ready for her to pick up when she leaves? Thank you." Without waiting for me to take his hand, Zavier grabs mine and pulls me up anyway.

This man has a thing about touching me and I'm trying to figure out if I like it or not. Mostly not.

It's not a big deal, I don't need the money, but having this particular croupier handling what's mine doesn't sit right with me. He's liable to take it and fuck off, never to be seen again. Well... only because I'd find his ass, slice him open a few times, then find a fun way to dispose of his body.

But... do I tell Zavier about his cheating, back-stabbing staff, or do I keep my mouth shut and let his empire crumble beneath him?

Decisions, decisions.

Fuck it, I'd rather lose some money than give Zavier a heads-up.

I follow Zavier, weaving through the various tables of blackjack, craps, and roulette. There are slot machines around the edges, all occupied by people waiting for spaces to open up at the tables.

My back pocket begins vibrating and I check the time—ten-thirty—before checking the caller ID.

Hallie.

She's messaged me at least once a day since we met, and even though I've been trying to keep my distance after nearly outing myself at her school the other day, she's a persistent little thing.

I don't want to ignore her again, because I have no doubt she'll try again another thirty times, so I decide Zavier can wait. Following him into his office was a bad idea anyway; there's no way we wouldn't have fucked if I went with him.

Trouble is, Zavier notices, quickly moving to my side and looking over my shoulder as I press to answer the call.

"Hey, Kid. Everything okay?" That feeling of being in constant worry for her well-being that Murphy explained to me is strong. I've never experienced anything like it.

"Yeah, just wondering if I can see you this weekend. I booked us in at the salon to get our nails done on Saturday afternoon an—"

"Kid, that sounds great." It doesn't, it sounds like torture, but Zavier is staring at me with an amused expression on his smug fucking face and I'm being stupid right now.

Again.

Letting my guard down when I really shouldn't be.

"But I can't really talk right now, I'll call you in the morning."

"Okay, Mom. Talk to you tomorrow." There's a little sadness in her tone at first, but it's quickly masked by a happy-go-lucky attitude and I can't help the strange warmth flooding my insides, allowing a tiny smile to tip my lips.

"Tomorrow." I end the call and look to Zavier, shrugging in a *what?* motion as he continues to stare at me with a stupidly sexy eyebrow raised.

"Who's Hallie then?"

"My real estate agent." I can't let him see Hallie means anything to me because he's the kinda sick fuck who would find a way to use it against me.

"At this time of night?" He clearly knows I'm lying, it's obvious in his amused tone. Sad story for him though; I won't cower under his penetrating hazel glare.

"What can I say? I inspire people to work all hours of the night." I keep my features neutral, shrugging, and do the only thing I can to change the subject—well, the only thing that doesn't involve getting stabby. "I thought we were gonna fuck..." There's a small pang in my stomach as the thought of Murphy crosses my mind, and as much as I would love to revisit that part of my past, I remind myself that they're both safe if I keep my distance.

"I like a lady who speaks her mind." Zavier laughs and holds out his hand for me to take. "I was going to offer you a drink first, but if you insist."

"I could go for a drink." Instead of taking his hand, I hold my head high and walk straight past him, toward the door I know leads to the back where his office is located.

This time, I don't need to wait for security to let me through the door. It's already unlocked and open as I approach so I decide to thank whoever's behind the cameras tonight with a wink.

"Are you always full of this much sass, Shadow?"

My palm is resting against the round knob of his office door when Zavier crowds my space from behind, pushing his rock-hard cock into the bottom of my back and reaching a hand around to my throat. His lips are against my ear, his breath tickling my skin, and my pulsing clit reminds me the last time I had an orgasm was two days ago, by my own hands... with Murphy on my mind.

Fuck!

He's safer without me—I need to remind myself of this more often than I'd like, like a broken fucking record.

"I'd be full of your cock too if you'd stop talking long enough to get the job done." I push my ass back into Zavier and it's followed by a deep rumble from his chest, which spurs me on.

Turning the knob, I push open the office door and grip Zavier's hand suddenly on my throat. I don't remove it, instead I keep hold of it at my throat and use it to drag him into the room behind me.

This really is not the best idea I've ever had, and I can use the excuse that I'm working and this is how I get close to Zavier, but it seems unfair to him, and especially Murphy.

Anyone say *self-saboteur?*

His grip tightens, his fingertips dig deeper, and my phone begins vibrating again in my back pocket. Like fate's way of intervening.

"Is that a vibrator in your pocket?" Zavier's lips move to a smile as he slides his palm over my ass.

I should ignore the call, but of course I don't. With a heavy sigh, I turn away from Zavier and pull my phone out of my pocket. Without looking, I answer and hold the phone to my ear.

"Yeah?"

"Hello to you, too."

Shit. Murphy.

"What's up?" I try to move away from Zavier, who has moved closer yet, his nose at my neck while I'm trying to keep my end of the conversation neutral. Zavier doesn't let up though, wrapping his other arm around my waist before cupping my pussy.

"She just told me you're going to get your nails done together on Saturday. Don't let her down." Murph's tone isn't like before, fun and jovial, there's a hint of disapproval in there and I think he's finally finding that anger I thought he'd pushed away.

I stamp my foot onto Zavier's because pushing at him isn't working.

"Ah, fuck! What was that for?"

"Seriously?" I can hear Murphy inhaling deeply and I'm about to respond, but he continues before I get a chance when I finally free myself of Zavier. "Like I said, just don't let her down."

Then he hangs up without a goodbye... again.

Murphy's angry with me again for whatever reason, Zavier is now sitting in his desk chair nursing a sore foot... and, apparently, I have an appointment to get my nails done with my daughter on Saturday.

I need to make peace with the fact that I can't run away from this—or slaughter it.

Either way, life has become a lot more complicated and I'll figure out a way to do this.

I have to.

CHAPTER ELEVEN

J

I can't fucking believe I'm getting my nails done.

What's the point, anyway? They'll just get ruined the first chance I get to spar at the gym. It's a complete and total waste of my time and gas money. And I mean, seriously… the price of gas is definitely not worth crossing over into the armpit of New York. That's right, I'm willingly going to New Jersey, and no matter how many times I've tried to talk myself out of this fucking predicament, it always comes back to one thing.

I have a daughter.

So, here I am, checking the time to make sure I'm not late to the fucking salon.

"J! I need your full attention on this. Got it?" My eyes snap up to Marco's glare. I know he's projecting his anger onto me because I'm the only one here and River would have his fucking balls if he ever spoke to her like this, but still... I'm having a crisis and Zavier's incompetent employees are ruining my morning.

"Got it, boss." Truth is, I missed a part of what he said but I'm pretty sure it started with bring that fucker to me and then slice his neck open from ear to ear.

Okay, fine, I may have made that second part up because that's actually what I want to do to him.

"You'll need to spend more time there. Get proof of his mishandling and outright cheating." If he could wear out marble with his pacing, he'd have a deep groove going at this rate.

Wait a fucking minute. What now?

"More time, sir?" I'm there twice a week, I'm not going more often than that.

"Yeah, I need you to give me undeniable proof so I can get what I need from Gallanos." A yapping Polo comes running into the office, sliding across the floor and almost knocking himself out against the bookshelf as he side paddles in an effort to correct his trajectory. With a yelp, he shakes his fur out and just as quickly as he arrived, he's in Marco's arms getting his full attention like a tiny baby human.

The head of the Mancini mob, who not only orders some gruesome jobs but executes them just the same, is standing here with a tiny ball of fur cuddled against his neck. I don't get it.

"Polo!" River Mancini walks in like she's owning a cat-walk, her slick, dark gray skirt hugs every curve of her body like a forties pin-up girl while her light salmon blouse gives away just enough cleavage to make my boss lose his grip on sanity.

This is my cue to get the fuck out.

"All right, Boss. I'll look into the thing and..." He's barely paying attention to me. Actually, by the way he's staring at his wife and having some sort of silent conversation with her, I'm guessing he's forgotten I'm even here.

"Later, Boss." I don't bother to say more except when I pass River and smirk. "Good luck with that." And by *that*, I mean, getting out of that office without her clothes getting ripped to pieces.

"My evil plan works every time." River's answer makes me chuckle. I fucking love this woman.

"Heard that. Come here." Speed walking out of his of-fice, I make sure I'm nowhere within ear shot before they start making porn music on his desk.

I guess I'll be seeing more of Zavier than I had planned.

"Hi! I'm Sophie, I'll be working with you today and the appointment said to have two stations next to each other, so Carrie will be at the station next to me. First off, do you have a color in mind?" Hallie looks at me expectantly, like my answer to this woman will solve world hunger. Ask me how to dismantle a gun or how to pack a body up into a square box without giving anything away and we're golden. Nail polish color? Who the fuck knows?

"Black." It's brief, but I see it. The woman's nose ticks up just enough to show me her snob and I resist the urge to punch her in the throat.

"Me too!" That's right, lady. I'm cool while you're just a cunt.

"Your dad's gonna kill me, you know that right? I thought thirteen-year old's were into pink and purple." The lady walks over to the middle of the salon where a revolving tower full of nail polish takes up a good chunk of the space. I'm watching her pick out not one but three different black nail polish bottles before she makes her way to the sink and washes her hands.

"Mom, that's your inner misogyny speaking. Girls don't have to wear pink or purple, we can wear whatever color we want." Inner misogyny? What the actual fuck is happening right now? I've defied the odds of sexism, fought—literally—my way up the ranks in the fucking mafia and lived to talk about it. I've cut off the balls of men groping me without my consent and ripped out the guts—intestines and all—of an asshole who thought I owed him and wanted to collect his loot between my legs.

The color of nail polish doesn't even make the top one hundred list of what I consider misogyny but... sure, I'll play the game.

"It's not about the color, Kid. It's about the perception of optimism. At thirteen, everything should be seen through rose-colored glasses. Black is reserved for reality and the truth is..." I lean in to whisper in her ear so the other pearl-clutching housewives don't shit an offended brick. "Reality sucks."

Sophie comes back with her coworker—Carrie, I assume. They couldn't be more different. Where Sophie holds a certain type of presence, like she's used to doing manicures for the Queen of England and not in a mall located next to one of our concrete dump sites, Carrie looks like she's not a minute older than fifteen. Sitting across the narrow table from Hallie, she pops her gum as she greets my daughter and I swear to fuck, I want to rip her tongue out for her unprofessionalism.

"Sorry." I didn't miss Sophie kicking Carrie on the side of her foot, prompting a mumbled apology.

"Okay, so before we begin I'll need to ask a couple of questions."

My back immediately straightens. I don't like questions. I don't fucking answer questions.

I raise a brow at Sophie, who recoils just enough for me to notice.

"Oh, come on, Mom. It'll be fun, I promise." There isn't a doubt in my mind that I'm going to regret this later.

"What are your questions?" Here we go. I'm not excluding the possibility of lying through my teeth.

Sophie takes a little card from inside the middle drawer of her station and clicks a pen, looking at me with wide eyes like a deer watching the bullet coming straight at her.

"Name and date of birth?" Fuck. Simple questions for anyone else, but a death warrant for me.

"Meaghan Bachmeier. June fifteenth, nineteen eighty-nine." She wants to ask me questions? Well, I'm not making it easy on her.

"Um, how do you spell that?" Slowly, I spell out my fake name, Hallie's wide eyes burning a hole in my profile. I'm afraid to face her, not exactly proud of this moment.

"Okay, so an email or telephone number so we can reach you?" Why the fuck would they need to reach me?

"Why? Are you going to call me to make sure my nails aren't chipped?" I'm snappy, I can't help it. I hate disappointing Hallie with secrets and lies this early on in our relationship.

"Um, no. It's just... standard... but... um, okay, we skip that." Smart girl. "Do you have any medical conditions or allergies we should know about?"

I just stare at her instead of answering. Do people actually give out their medical history to complete strangers just to get their nails painted? "No."

"Oh, good. Okay, so, have you ever had your..." her voice trails off as she carefully places her hands under mine and inspects my fingers and nails. "Nails done?" Sherlock here just figured out the answer to her own question.

"No."

Next to me, Hallie has been answering the same questions, except she's eager to give out her information. I guess when you have nothing to hide, the truth is easy to give.

"Well, there are few options here. Acrylic, gel, or a simple nail polish. Which would you prefer?" My head snaps to the side, my eyes narrowed on Hallie, who is grinning from one ear to the other.

"She'll just have a regular polish. I'll get the gel." Hallie winks at me like she gets that this is a whole new ballgame for me and I'm not excited about it.

"What's the difference between the three styles?" I don't like choosing without knowing my options.

"Gel will last longer and overall look better." Hallie shrugs like she's an expert on this and she just gave me some free advice.

My head cocked to the side, I actually consider doing the same thing as my daughter, but I'm guessing there's some kind of catch to it and I have zero patience for unnecessary tasks.

"It's a little harder to take off but if you soak a ball of cotton in acetone, wrap it around your nails with aluminum foil after filing off the top-coat, and let it work its magic for thirty minutes, you're golden."

I arch a brow at my kid, making sure she reads my absolute disinterest in doing any of that shit she just mentioned.

There are a lot of assumptions in her explanation, like me owning acetone or cotton balls or fucking aluminum foil. I don't cook and take-out doesn't require any of that shit.

Hallie turns back to Sophie, a bright smile on her plump little lips like we're sharing a private joke and mock-whispers. "Like I said, she'll have the regular polish."

I really like this kid. Murphy did a great fucking job, but I'm pretty sure she's amazing regardless.

My biggest mistake was thinking Sophie was finished with her interrogations.

She was not.

"Would like your nails reshaped? Maybe elongated? I can sculpt them rounded, square, rounded-square—"

"You just said that."

"No, it's not totally the same thing. One is rounded, the other squared and the third option is a little of both." I blink and I want to shoot myself in the head for even caring about her answer.

"Right." She doesn't stop there, though.

"Also, we have oval, stiletto, and coffin." Did she just say...

"Coffin? As in the resting place for the dead?" What the fuck parallel dimension did I just walk into?

Sophie perks up and I hate to break it to her, but the only coffins I'm interested in are the ones that I burn to ashes when I need evidence gone.

"Yes! So they're kind of like this..." she shows me her pointed nails, which should probably be classified as deadly weapons, before placing a wooden stick with one end flattened out right on the edge of her nail. "Except it's clipped straight instead of pointy." Ah, to be young and naïve.

"I'm guessing yours are stilettos?" Also a good replacement for a weapon. At my question, Sophie grins like I just gave her the fucking moon.

"Yes, exactly."

"No, thank you." See? I can be polite. "Just one question though... how do you do everyday activities with your nails?"

Sophie beams at my question, leaning in like she's about to hand over the secrets of youth and good fortune.

"Jewels not tools." She winks as she utters her words, the spark in her eyes the only clue that those words are supposed to mean something to me.

They absolutely do not.

"Rounded for me, please," is Hallie's answer, and by the look of her nails right now, I'm guessing it's what she usually gets done. Fuck me. When I was thirteen, my dad would have kicked my ass if I had come home with manicured nails.

I decided to ignore this whole process and just enjoy this time with my daughter while I hand over the reins to Sophie and her wooden stick pushing back on my cuticles. Does it hurt? Not really, but it definitely doesn't feel good.

"So, tell me something. What does your dad do for work?" I'm watching her every move, every tick, making sure I don't get any other version than the truth to my questions.

"I don't know, something about distribution of something or other at the port. I think he's like an accountant or something? He works a lot with numbers on his computer but only goes to the office in the mornings while I'm at school." One of her shoulders rises in a shrug, clearly not having any more information for me.

"So he's got time to take care of you. Smart." I can't help but wonder if he's, in any way, associated with the Irish mob. After all, we were raised and bathed in it over here and I can't imagine them just looking the other way, especially if they know Hallie is mine. I'm going to need to find out for sure because if my suspicions are correct, it's going to complicate things.

"Yeah, I guess he's doing his best, you know?" Her tentative side-eye tells me there's more to that comment.

"I'm sure he is." I'm waiting for the rest of her concerns to hit me in the gut and she doesn't disappoint.

"There are just things he can't help me with, you know?" I think I'm supposed to be understanding something here, and when Carrie starts humming at Hallie like she gets it, I want to throat-punch her too.

"Daddies do not like Red Ribbongate."

What the actual fuck is this chick talking about? Also, why? Why is she even talking?

My glare is so potent, she visibly recoils and snaps her mouth shut.

"You're going to have to spell it out, Hals, I'm not following here." I hate being the last to understand.

Hallie leans in and whispers softly, "I got my first period a few months ago and, well, I freaked out. Then he freaked out. Then we spent two hours watching videos."

I freeze, the image of Murphy and Hallie looking up shit on the internet to—I'm hoping and supposing—help her use a tampon or a sanitary pad flashes through my mind on a reel. My second reaction is to laugh outright. In front of me, Sophie gasps and, swear to fucking Jesus and the saints, one hand clutches onto her nonexistent pearls.

"Relax. Your mind went way dark there." Also, mind your own fucking business.

"But you're here now so everything is perfect. It was my birthday wish and it's come true."

"Aww." I was about to have feelings, right there in my chest again, but Carrie Whothefuckaskedyou interrupts with her little show of emotions.

"Yeah, I've never been happier." I hear Hallie cooing just as I bring my mouth closer to Carrie's station, forgetting that I'm in a public place surrounded by daytime people who have no fucking clue what happens to their kind in the middle of the night.

"I know how to bury bodies so no one can find them. Interrupt us again and I'll show you."

This time, both Sophie and Carrie gasp, their hands frozen, their mouths doing weird fish-like movements, and I realize I may have given them a little too much of myself.

"True crime TV, amiright?" I grin like it's all just a joke, Hallie giggling beside me, not fazed in the least while the girls clear their throats and pretend I didn't just threaten to kill and bury them the next time they open their mouths.

I'm pretty sure this was my first and last manicure and I'm not really sorry about it. Next time, we'll have a girls' day my way.

CHAPTER TWELVE

J

"Ohmygod! That was wild. Bridget is gonna be so pissed when I show her these pics." Hallie scrolls back and forth over the images I've just taken of her sitting on my bike, her silver, glittery phone case sparkling in her small hands when the beams from passing headlights flash over it.

I chuckle, warmth radiating through me at her beautiful little smile that I put there. Me. I made her smile this big. It's a sensation I'm not used to, but damn if I don't like making this girl happy.

"Come on, Kid, your dad's probably inside wearing the carpet down."

"Nah, he's been peeking through the curtains since we pulled up." *Of course he has.* She begins skipping up the short path toward her front door, which opens as soon as she places a foot on the porch step.

The security light above the entrance shines brightly in the evening sky, highlighting the breathtaking man now standing there with our precious daughter in his arms. He places a kiss on the top of her head before she unfurls herself from him and turns to face me.

"You coming in for coffee, Mom?"

I realize I haven't moved, just watching the scene unfold in front of me, that warmth from before still present. Murphy scowls at the question and I can see the war on his face. He's angry with me again and doesn't want me here, but he also doesn't want to make Hallie unhappy by telling me to go. The decision is mine though, he won't make it for me and that much is clear.

"I don't think—"

"Please?" This girl... it's like she has a direct link to what I thought was a permanently broken heart. As though with every word spoken to me she's finding ways to pull it back together.

"Okay. One cup."

Clapping her hands together, she turns and skips inside, leaving Murphy and me in a stare-off. I sigh, deciding to suck it up. The anger I had initially expected from him when I first saw him was clearly delayed, and it's nothing I don't deserve, so I'll deal with it.

For her.

Murphy tries to block the entrance but I move past him, sliding through the doorway and brushing my arm against his. Then the minty smell that is all Murphy hits me, and fuck me, my insides are raging for more of him. A touch on the arm could barely be classified as foreplay, but I remember the way he used to make me feel, in another lifetime, and being this close to him is becoming a problem for my tingling clit and nipples, now begging for attention.

Thank fuck for padded bras because it's warm enough in this house that I couldn't blame my erect nipples on the cold.

In the kitchen, Hallie is madly tapping away on her cell when it starts ringing.

"Hey, Hils! Hang on a sec, I'm just with my mom." She moves to stand beside me, showing me the young dark-haired girl on the other side of the screen.

"Hi." The girl waves, a shy smile on her face, and I tip my head in acknowledgement before Hallie puts the screen back to herself.

"I'm going to my room to talk to Hilary. She's been away with her family for like, two weeks so we neeeed to catch up." And just like that, I'm easily forgotten and she's practically bouncing from the room then up the stairs, muttering something about not finding her social media posts.

It would seem my daughter is a whirlwind, and I'm not totally sure if she still wants me to stay now that she's busy.

"Don't be offended, she's only had her phone for a few months so it's still a novelty to video chat with her friends." Murphy has a sad smile on his lips, less of the angry from before, but I still see it in his eyes.

"Have I done something wrong? I was under the impression we'd talked this all out already." Not one to hold in my true feelings on a subject, I figure now is as good a time as any to bring up this new awkwardness between us.

Moving to pour a couple of coffees, Murph shakes his head, a smirk tipping the corner of his mouth as he prepares mine how I like it.

"Here." He passes me a steaming hot fresh coffee, then leans against the workspace opposite me, his palms against the countertop. "Why would you think you've done something wrong?"

Good question.

"I don't, but you've been an ass the last few times we've talked, and when I agreed to come in for coffee I thought steam was gonna come outta your ears."

"Fair point." He sighs, looking to the floor. "It's a me thing. Nothing for you to worry about, Jaybear."

"I call bullshit. You can't even look me in the eye, so I know you're talking outta your asshole, Murph."

Maybe I read the situation last weekend all wrong, but I'm a smart woman. I know I didn't. Murphy kissed me, and it meant a lot to both of us. More than I'm ready to willingly admit to myself right now, but that doesn't make it any less true. And now this crap? No.

After placing my coffee on the surface behind me, I move toward him, so close but not quite touching. With our height difference, he now has no choice but to look me in the eye.

"What's wrong?" I don't really have the right to be making him answer me like this, but I hate not knowing things. Information, in any situation, is important, it can make or break an outcome, and since we're clearly going to be in each other's lives to some extent—forever—I kinda feel like it's my responsibility to know everything.

His brown orbs are stormy as they lock with mine, his hair flops forward and the urge to push it back is strong. I almost move to do just that, when he opens his mouth to speak.

Instead, he sighs again, but his eyes don't shift. Our breaths are so close, they're mingling together, creating a warmth on the outside to match the growing one I have on the inside.

"I don't know if I can do this, Jaybear. It's too hard."

Not what I was expecting, but I also understand. I'm a danger to them.

Fuck if I don't hate it though.

"Life's hard, Murph. We deal with it and move the fuck on." I may understand, but it doesn't mean I'm willing to let either of them go now that I know I have a daughter.

"I mourned you once before, for us, for her, for the life we could've had, and now that you're back, I let that dream crawl out of its grave. I shouldn't have assumed you'd want that life, or even still be single. Because of course you're not. I just..." He finds a way to avoid my gaze, looking to the ceiling and bringing a hand up, cupping the back of his neck.

"To assume makes an ass out of you and me, Murph. How many times did we hear that? Never assume anything." He brings his eyes back down to meet mine again, defeated understanding clear in his gaze, and I want to beat it out of him. "But in no way, shape, or form, am I in a relationship." I wave both hands in kind of a surrender. I have no fucking clue why I felt the need to make sure he knows I'm single, but he returns my small smile. "Can we just drop all the crap and get on like we were beginning to before?"

Murphy raises a brow, a mischievous glint in his eye now. "Where we were beginning to before... like when I brushed against you?" He brings a hand up to my face, stroking his knuckles across my cheek. The touch is fucking electric and my will to stay away from this man for his safety is slowly crumbling.

Let's be fair, I'm not really expending much effort on trying to hold it together.

"Or like when I kissed you?" Leaning down, his breath fans across my lips, which are barely a paper's width away from his.

I don't back down, don't move away, waiting for him to close that small distance between us, because then I can at least tell myself I tried to stay away, to stop what was happening.

The kitchen is deathly silent, Murphy's thick cock has closed the distance between us and he's now pressed up against my stomach. His hand is still on my cheek, palm down now, his thumb moving back and forth. His eyes are fixed on mine, and it would be so easy to get lost in those again. Our breaths are heavy as we both contemplate whether this is okay, whether this is what the other wants for sure. Somehow, I must've moved closer, because now my breasts are pressed up against him, the friction making walking away from this damn near impossible.

"Fuck it." Murphy makes the move. His hands cup my face, his tongue demands entrance, and his oh-so-soft lips are causing a bonfire inside my brain. It's terrifyingly perfect and I grip my arms around his neck, lifting myself up his body and wrapping my legs around his waist.

The phrase climbing someone like a tree has never been truer.

Moving his hands from my face, Murph grips onto my ass, kneading the muscles and causing more friction against my pussy with every squeeze. I'm basically dry humping him as if we were still teenagers and I couldn't give two shits. The last time I was this turned on was... well, with Murphy.

"Daaad!" Hallie's elongated word suggests she wants something and I immediately unfurl myself from my childhood sweetheart. Fuck, I've gone soft since he's been back. Or since I've been back. Whatever...

Murphy grins at me, giving me one last kiss before smacking my ass and picking up his coffee just as Hallie makes it down the stairs and into the kitchen.

Holy shit, that was hot.

"Hils just told me that new movie we wanted to watch is on Netflix. Can we watch it, please?" Hallie seems none the wiser about what was just going on in here, and when she's rooting through the cupboard for fuck knows what, Murph winks at me.

"Of course, baby girl. You're on popcorn, I'll make milkshakes, and—"

"Ooh, Mom can grab the blankets and pillows. They're in the cupboard under the stairs." Clapping her hands together, which seems to be her thing, she pulls out a bag of popcorn before reaching to another cupboard and pulling out a large bowl. "You *are* gonna stay for the movie, right?"

Her pleading eyes as she stops what she's doing and puts all her attention on me are going to stay with me for an eternity. I couldn't let this girl down if I tried.

"Sure." I shrug, and she grips my waist, squeezing me before getting back to organizing the popcorn. "I'll get right on that."

Murphy wags his brows as I'm leaving the room and memories of playing under the blankets and watching movies together as kids hits me in a wave of nostalgia. He'd often join my mom and me on movie nights like this when our dads were out on various jobs.

I fire off a quick text to the Reapers group chat, letting them know I won't be back to the clubhouse as I had planned this evening. Glitch has some info on the Mr. Wright guy that he wanted to share, but whatever it is can wait 'til tomorrow.

My soft ass is gonna be spending the next couple of hours under a blanket watching I don't even care what.

Time with my girl is priceless.

And maybe Murphy too, but I'm not dissecting those feelings just yet.

CHAPTER THIRTEEN

J

Thirteen-year-old girls take up a lot of space.

As the credits to the movie begin to roll, I'm acutely aware of Hallie sleeping across the couch with half her body sprawled out on her father and the other half on me. I got the feet part of this deal while her father is the pillow to her head. I guess I need to work myself up to that privilege.

Or not. Logically, I should be disappearing into the shadows and making sure they stay far away from the bloodshed that will ensue if the Irish mob ever finds me. If they haven't already.

"She's conked out. I'll take her up to bed." I don't move an inch as Murph picks up the corner of his blanket and pulls it, slow and easy, off of him, then Hallie, who doesn't even stir an inch.

This is all new to me. The movie watching, the cuddling, the family setup. Murph, though? It's like second nature. He knows just how to move to avoid waking her, just where to place his arms as he picks her up and carries her off to her room.

I can't stop staring. It's more fascinating than the fucking two-hour movie I just forced myself to watch. About halfway up the stairs, he stops just before his head disappears above the drywall and nods his head, telling me to follow him.

I hesitate for just a second, not quite sure how good of an idea it is to get even more attached to this life, to this idea that I could have a family again. I could love my childhood sweetheart and the daughter I thought never survived. But my logic is bitch-slapped by my visceral need to participate in whatever routine they share. *Have* shared since that day I ran from the bloody corpses of my parents and my baby, cutting the umbilical cord and never looking back.

Well, except for that diner. Every fucking year, I mourned the death of my baby, spending an entire twenty-four hours allowing my vaulted down heart to crack, to come out and revisit the most painful day of my life.

I wish I could tell that terrified, confused, sixteen-year-old girl to... do something different. But even as I look back, I can't imagine carrying a dead body with me as I ran for my life through the streets of New Jersey covered in blood. Going to a hospital was out of the question, they had the Irish on auto dial. A church? They were owned by the mob. There was nothing but Manhattan left for me, where a rival mob would welcome good intel in exchange for safety.

By the time we reach Hallie's bedroom, I'm thinking of a million ways to make this work, but as soon as we enter her private little space, all thoughts of the Italians and the Irish disappear completely. I'm in her world, where the two biggest walls are essentially bookshelves, half filled with books, the other half with stuffed animals and trinkets. Her desk is in the corner of the two giant shelves with her laptop neatly closed and put away, her school books piled high.

Murphy gently places her in the middle of her king-size bed, half of it inside the nook of the bookshelf. She mumbles something about love and daddy and I watch, fascinated, as Murph bends down and places his lips on her forehead, wishing her sweet dreams full of fictional book boyfriends.

What now? Making a mental note to ask what the ever-loving fuck that was about, I jolt in surprise when his hand touches mine, pulling me closer to Hallie's fast asleep form.

"Tell her goodnight." It's like he's teaching me the basics of being a mom and I'm already failing.

My eyes fixed on Hallie, I blink, my chest heating with some weird feeling of pride and... love, I think. I remember this. It's how I felt every time I was with Murphy Gallagher, the good Irish boy from down the street. It's how I felt about my parents every time they hugged me.

With shaky hands and a heart trying to gallop its way out of my ribcage, I bend at the waist and place my lips on her forehead. In that one specific moment, I have an epiphany, the clarity of my entire existence comes into view in the forefront of my mind and everything... every single thing... is simple.

I'm a mother. She's mine. Nothing else in this world could possibly come between us.

Stranger than the emotions that have taken permanent residence in my heart, are the tears threatening to fall down my cheeks and onto hers. No, I can't do that.

Taking in a deep breath, I find the strength to rise back up and step away from the perfection that is asleep in her gigantic bed.

"It's huge, isn't it?" Murphy's voice is suddenly so close, his lips grazing the outer shell of my ear, and I know he's not talking about the bed. "This feeling every time you look at her?"

I can't speak so I just nod, because he's right, it's bigger than anything I've ever experienced in my life. Bigger, even, than life itself.

"How do you live with it? I mean... how can you contain it?" My question seems strange but it's like my entire existence is now focused on her and only her. How do parents do it? Have a life outside of this love?

"You don't. Everything you do revolves around her and her needs. When she's a baby, as a toddler, as a child, and now as a teenager. You just evolve with her and adapt to whatever it is she needs from you." His lips land on the side of my neck and linger there long enough to have my heartbeat slamming against my chest again. "Mostly, you give her love. It's all she needs, really."

Suddenly, I wonder if he's still talking about Hallie as he turns me around in his arms and brings our foreheads together until we're inside our own private bubble. "All any of us need... is love."

For the first time since they've been back in my life, I allow myself to lower my guard and just bask in the warmth of these foreign emotions. Not foreign because I've never felt love, but because it's been so long that I have to remind my brain that it's possible.

Losing a child, no matter the circumstances or the age, is the most traumatizing experience possible. Yes, my parents' brutal murder broke something inside me, but seeing my baby's lifeless body lying in a pool of my own blood destroyed every single part of me. Working in the shadows of the mafia, killing and fighting for your life, is nothing compared to those couple of hours trapped inside a closet, trying to survive the loss of everyone I loved.

Yet, standing here with Murphy's hands centering me as our daughter sleeps safely and comfortably in her bed just two feet away from us is like a magnet bringing the broken pieces of my heart back together.

Murphy brings his soft lips to mine with a ghost of a kiss, barely a physical touch but with the emotional weight of a tsunami. When he pulls away, my lids are heavy with lust and need but as I focus on the sight of him, it's the smirk dancing at the corner of his lips that brings back memories of us from more than a decade ago.

"Come on, Jaybear." With my hand firmly trapped in his palm, he leads me to the corner of the bookshelf and plugs in a nightlight. The sudden appearance of stars and planets on the ceiling is mesmerizing. It's like Hallie has her own observatory right here in her bedroom.

"Wow." Yeah, real original, that reaction.

"She used to get night terrors when she was a toddler and this helped a little." Fuck, I missed so much... everything, really.

That thought provokes a ball of hatred in my gut and the urge to dig up the men who killed my parents and kill them all over again is overwhelming. Instead, I allow Murphy to lead us outside the room and down the stairs until we're back in the kitchen.

"Her room is big, and all those books?" I need to know more about her, learn her quirks and loves and dislikes.

"When I bought this house, it was badly in need of renovations. The only reason I could afford it was because it was a foreclosure. Plus, my parents and I negotiated the price based on the work it needed." Taking out the tea bags and a kettle, Murphy makes us a pot as our ancestors taught us. None of this American shit with water in the microwave.

The kitchen sink isn't piled up with dishes, the faux-marble counters don't have a single spot of dirt on them, and the floors aren't littered with crumbs. In other words, these two have a system and it works. They take care of each other. When I was a kid, my mother did everything and expected me to learn her ways while my father "took care of business". I didn't know it back then, but I do today. He was working for the Irish and putting us all in danger.

Sitting behind the breakfast bar that is basically a prolonged part of the kitchen counter, my breathing returns to something more natural, less frenzied. More controllable.

"Did you do all the work yourself?" I can't deny I'm impressed. Not because he's a single dad—women have been taking on the role of provider and nurturer since the beginning of time—but because he does it so naturally and so effortlessly. At least, that's how it seems from the outside looking in.

"God no. I had a lot of help. My parents took care of Hallie while I got the house fixed enough that we could live here. The plumbing was in bad shape and the electrical system was downright dangerous. But it was already a big house, I just broke down a wall upstairs to give Hallie a room that's the size of two." The kettle whistles just as Murphy hands me a cup and a spoon. It's been so long since someone, anyone, actually took care of me that I'm having a hard time just being and enjoying the calm. Just letting him do this one thing. Filling the pot with hot water, we wait for a few minutes for the tea to darken before pouring just over three quarters into our cups then adding a splash of milk. It's like riding a bicycle, it's shit you don't forget.

Once he's finished, my brain goes back to what he was saying earlier.

"You did the plumbing and electrical work yourself?" Murphy is about five months older than me so we were the same age when Hallie was born... sixteen.

"Nah. I bought the house once I got my first stable job at the garage, working during the day and taking night courses at the community college. On the weekends I'd fix her up with my uncles and their friends." My spine tingles, and not in the best way, as I bring my cup to my lips and look up at him above the rim.

"Uncles and friends, huh?" He's being vague and I fucking know why.

"Yeah, Jaybear. I had help because doing it alone wasn't possible. And yes, it was a non-bloodline family that made sure we had a roof over our heads. Gave me a job, helped me with college." On the outside, I'm calm and collected, but on the inside I'm thinking of a thousand ways to grab

Hallie and Murphy and get the fuck away from everyone here.

"Murph..." My voice is barely a whisper, like just thinking about the repercussions might manifest them in this very kitchen.

Putting his cup down, he's by my side with his hands on my cheeks, forcing me to look up at him and only him.

"You're not in danger here. The Irish? Their beef was with your father, not you and certainly not Hallie, so you can't go there." The sincerity in his deep, soulful brown eyes does things to me. Gives me hope, somehow.

Until I remember.

"No, Murph. They kno—" In one quick move, his lips are on mine and his tongue is sweeping inside my mouth, tasting and licking and fucking like he owns a part of me. The part that rules my libido and my heart.

My hands latch onto his t-shirt, fingers curling until the fabric is imprisoned inside my fist as I pull him closer, closer, closer. My ass is on the counter, my legs wrapped tightly around his waist as he palms the back of my head with one hand and digs his fingers into the flesh of my thighs like my leather pants aren't even there.

"Come upstairs with me, J. I need you." A better person would have hesitated. A better person would have put everyone's safety before her pussy's needs.

It's clear to say, I'm not that better person because I don't even answer, just grunt like words are too much to deal with and the only thing I'm aware of right now is him and all of these clothes between us.

Stepping back, Murphy guides me to my feet as we make our way out of the kitchen, down the hall, and up the stairs without an ounce of shame or an inch to separate us. We're back to our teenage selves, our libidos dictating every one of our moves. Our mouths hungry for the taste of the other, our bodies starved.

We're losing clothes as we walk, my sweater, his t-shirt... gone. My leathers and his jeans, which are gaping open at the crotch as his dick tries to pop out, are the only things left between us as my pussy begs for attention. Murphy has the sense to slow down as we pass Hallie's room, but I swear our breathing is loud enough to wake the dead.

As soon as we close the door to his bedroom on the opposite side of the floor, we're back to being teenagers, searching out ways to touch each other.

"Fuck, J. I've missed everything about you."

I push him away, smirking as he stumbles back with surprise etched all over his face.

I'm not letting him go but I need my clothes off and there's no way he can be faster than me. It doesn't take him long to realize that I'm all in tonight as he lets himself fall on the bed before propping himself up on his elbows and watching every move I make.

I don't make it a habit to strip down as a method of seduction but this is Murphy Gallagher, the love of my life, the father of my child. I'm not J the Shadow, right now. I'm Jordyn O'Neill and my only goal is to please the man in front of me.

That's what he is. Gone is the teen with the strong-yet-lanky features. Gone is the smooth surface of a boy's jaw and chest. Gone are the insecure gestures of innocence.

Murphy is all man. Strong. Confident. Virile.

Mine.

My leathers are now somewhere behind me, my bra could be hanging from the ceiling fan for all I know, and the only thing I have on are my panties, which sit low on my hips as my pussy increasingly wets them with my need.

As my gaze falls on his dick, I lick my lips, watching the head peek out with interest and curiosity.

"Back then, you were my gift. Right here and now? You're my salvation." Too deep into my lust to register his words, I drop to my knees, right between his thighs with my hands on the waistband of his jeans, urging him to lift his hips so I can pull off his clothes. It's not like he's going to fight me on this.

Thirty seconds later, his dick is in my hand, my lips sucking at the head, and I'm loving the sounds coming from his mouth. They're desperate, filthy words that make me want to force the orgasm right out of him. Take it for myself, taste him in the most basic of ways.

With my fingers wrapped around the base of his cock, I lift my gaze to his as he watches, awe clear in his soulful eyes.

He watches me take inch by delicious inch of his cock into my mouth, my tongue flat enough that I can make room for his thick dick as the head knocks at the back of my throat. We lock eyes, which is how I can read every emotion running through his features. It's how I can see the possession that settles as I make a slight choking sound just for his pleasure. It's why I don't flinch when he's suddenly sitting up straighter, his fingers clasped around my hair as he pushes me down, hard, forcing the filthy sounds out of me.

Murphy Gallagher is in complete control, directing this power play and turning the tables so that his pleasure becomes my pleasure, too. Pulling me away and off his cock, he traps me with my head angled up toward the ceiling, saliva coating my bottom lip and breaths coming in and out of my lungs in a staccato rhythm.

"I've never seen you on your knees, J. It suits you." My lip curls on instinct, being in a submissive pose has never been on my wish-list but, for some reason I can't explain, I don't move. Murphy reads me, his eyes bouncing from one eye to the other, down to my mouth, and back up to my eyes, a satisfied grin on those delectable lips of his.

"Do you know what suits me better?" I let my tongue slide across my bottom lip, collecting all the leftover moisture from when his cock was fucking my mouth before sinking my teeth down and grinning.

"I can't wait to hear it."

"My pussy riding your dick." His fingers tense around the loose strands of my hair, almost painfully, getting my attention instantly.

"Don't be crude, J. You can't kiss your daughter with a filthy mouth like that." Without letting me go, he pulls us up to a standing position until we're face to face. Nose to nose. Mouth to hungry mouth.

"Murphy Gallagher..." I cluck my tongue at him like he's just disappointed me. "Nobody said anything about kissing our daughter." Fighting against his hold, I welcome the pain as my lips feather touch his. "I'm talking about fucking." Reaching down, I push two of my fingers into my pussy and make sure to coat them with my cum before bringing them up to our barely-touching mouths. "I'm talking about this." With my drenched fingers smearing myself all over his lips, I grin at the animalistic growl that comes from deep in his throat.

Two seconds later, I'm thrown onto the bed, my panties ripped right off, and a cock buried so deep inside me it almost hurts.

"I am nothing but your servant." And serve me well, he does.

For about one minute before he stops.

"What the fuck, Murphy?" My hips are seeking him out, forcing him to move his cock, to fuck me. To give me something.

"I changed my mind." *He did what now?*

Pulling out, he has the gall to grin and wink at me before sliding down my body, spreading my legs and throwing them over his shoulders as his mouth molds to my cunt and his tongue fucks me like he owns me.

I forget all about my control issues or the need to dominate on any given day as he feasts on my body. With both of his hands grabbing onto my ass cheeks, he buries his face between my legs, eating his second dinner of the night, protein and all.

My hips are thrusting, seeking more of him, more of his oh-so-fucking-talented tongue. Wanting more, more lips and fingers and, goddammit, I want his dick inside me and I fucking want it now!

"I swear to Christ, Murphy, if you don't fuck me right now, I'll scream like a goddamn banshee." I won't. There's no fucking way I'm traumatizing my kid with the unerasable image of her father's face going to town on her mother.

Slowly, torturously so, he pulls away just enough to flick my clit then drags his tongue down my slit until he parts my lips again and laps up everything I'm giving him. "No need to scream, Jaybear. Come on my face and I'll fuck any part of your body you want."

Music. To. My. Fucking. Ears.

It's like his words brought on the onslaught, giving me permission to let it all go. My hands fly up and behind my head, latching onto the headboard as my hips bounce off the mattress, seeking him out.

Humming inside me, he digs the pads of his fingers into the flesh of my ass and slurps—actually fucking slurps—up my cum just as my orgasm begins to burn through my veins and take over my entire system. For all I know, he's suffocating down there, but my mind is too far gone to actually care. Just as my big *O* begins to overwhelm me, I clamp a hand down onto my mouth and try my fucking hardest not to wake up the neighbors.

Truth be told, I don't give a single flying fuck about the neighbors, I just don't want to wake up Hallie.

"That's my good girl." Licking a path up my cunt, over my clit, and across the skin of my belly, he stops briefly on my tits and sucks them both into his mouth, moaning like he's tasting some French delicacy as it comes out of the oven. When he reaches my mouth, his tongue demands entrance as his dick slides right into me and straight to the hilt.

We're skin against sweaty skin, mouth against mouth, and our most intimate parts are finally reunited as though no time has passed.

I've had a lot of fucking men in my lifetime, but only one has ever been Murphy.

The frantic need is now gone and I'm only left with all of these fucking emotions. He's not fucking me from behind and I'm not fucking him from the top. We're eye to eye, equals in our need to pleasure each other, both eager to give something that has only ever belonged to the other.

"You taste better than I remembered. The fantasy of you pales in comparison to the reality of us."

There's nothing I can say that could possibly match his words. He's the romantic, always has been, while I'm the pragmatic one. It works, I think. He says sweet words to me and I absorb them like a lovesick sponge.

Fucking me, slow and steady, he pulls out almost all the way before pushing back inside, hard and determined. His eyes never look anywhere else but at me. My eyes, my lips, my nose, my neck. We don't speak—he's said it all—we just take it all in, remember it all, get lost in the moment.

Then he bites his lip and his breathing gets erratic, his eyes become unfocused and his hips speed up just the tiniest bit. And I know. He's about to come inside me. For the first time in thirteen years, Murphy Gallagher is going to come inside my pussy as a grown man.

With one forearm holding his weight right beside my head, he brings his other one to cup my cheek as he fucks me in earnest. In and out, fast, deep, full of need like no other. My thighs spread even wider, my hips meeting him thrust for thrust as he grunts every time the head of his dick connects with my deepest, darkest trigger. My breath hitches, my back arching into him as his fingers dig deeper into my cheek, almost to the point of pain.

I welcome it, I crave it, even, and he gives me everything I need and want.

"Jordyn." It's only one word.

My name.

He said my name and that's as close as he could ever get to saying he loves me.

"Murphy."

It's all we need to fall into the abyss. His cum fills me up in violent spurts and frantic thrusts. The sound of slippery, slapping skin is all I can hear besides our breaths coming in long and deep as we try so fucking hard not make any noise.

But it's okay, we don't need anything more than this.

This moment.

This perfect, unviolated moment of bliss. We give this gift to each other because in the morning, reality will drop on us like a fucking bomb drops from a drone.

Stealthy and deadly.

CHAPTER FOURTEEN

J

"That's weird. Nothing at all?" Marco leans back in his leather chair, running his fingers over the dark stubble on his chin.

"No. Glitch is still on it, but so far, Mr. Wright seems to be a bit of a ghost. Meaning his connections to Zavier are currently unknown. We do know that Mr. Wright has been in the casino every Monday and Friday, without fail, since it opened—according to the CCTV footage Glitch found. Shoo's been trying to tail him outside of the casino, but for an old dude, he's a slippery fucker." I sip the whiskey Marco handed me when we came into his office, sitting on the couch in the corner of the room. Usually, I'd stand; opting to get straight to business then leave when I'm done, but today, I'm tired.

I'm drained.

Inside, I'm a fucking wreck, if I'm honest with myself. Murphy's been calling and texting non-stop since I left in the early hours of yesterday morning and I've texted Hallie some bullshit excuse about work keeping me busy.

"I have no doubt that you and your Reapers will figure something out soon, J. It's only a matter of time."

"Yeah. Meanwhile, I'll be heading there in a few hours, see if I can't work my magic." I sigh, sipping at my glass of whiskey again. The burn as it slides down my throat is bliss, but I can't indulge fully. I need to keep my headspace sharp—or as sharp as it can be with my emotions running rampant.

The pitter patter of tiny paws sounds from the hall and I know this conversation is about to come to an end. Because where Polo goes, River goes, so she'll no doubt be following close behind the little pomeranian.

"I should go." I move to stand just as Polo runs into the room and jumps up onto my knees, having a good sniff and wagging his tail, hoping for some attention. Stroking under his chin, I chuckle at the persistent pooch.

"Looks like someone wants you to stay." River's soft tone reaches my ears as she enters the office, heading straight over to sit on Marco's lap. She looks over her shoulder and kisses his cheek before setting her gaze on me. "What's wrong?" Her eyes narrow and she raises a knowing brow. It's impossible to keep secrets from this woman. Like she has a sixth sense to anything abnormal.

"Nothing. I'm good. Just about to leave, got a job." Ruffling Polo's fur on his head, I do actually stand this time, reaching to grab my helmet from the floor by my feet.

River purses her lips and her eyes narrow further, and I know she doesn't believe me, but I'm hoping she drops it. She's aware that I'm not exactly the "sharing is caring" kinda woman.

"Catch ya later, Boss." I tip my head to Marco, then focus on River, giving her an acknowledging nod also. "River."

I knew it was too good to be true; just as I'm out of the room and reaching for the front door, the pattering feet on the marble floor are followed by the soft tones of River Fox-Mancini's voice.

"J, hold up."

Internally, and okay, externally too, I roll my eyes and turn to face my boss's wife. We all know she's the one that really runs the show these days. Without her, Marco would be fucked. She's the heart of the entire fucking New York mafia and none of us would have it any other way.

"What's up, Riv?"

"I think you should be answering that question, not me. Your vibes and your aura are all off kilter, J. Talk to me." She bends down to lift Polo into her arms, tickling the fur on his tiny head and looking at me with concern in her sparkling green eyes.

"Seriously? No. Nothing to talk about anyway." I shake my head and shrug, but my façade is useless against River.

"I call bullshit."

I can't help but laugh because she heard me say this so many times to Marco when I was his second—and since then—and now she's using my own words on me. Sly hippie.

"It's a me thing, nada for you and Marco to worry about. Really, it's fine." I reach for the door again, but she moves in front of me, holding it closed.

"Liar."

She's using *me* against me. Short and simple responses are all she's giving me—usually my M.O., not hers.

There's a stare-off for what feels like longer than the few minutes it actually is, until River's stern face breaks and she huffs.

"Come on, J. I know something's up. Why don't we get Stefano to make us some snacks and we'll grab some coffee?" Polo wriggles in her arms at the mention of snacks, and she gently lowers him to the floor before he moves his little legs as fast as he can toward the kitchen.

"Really, Riv? Snacks and a coffee for girl-time?" It's my turn to raise an eyebrow at her because she really thinks this is about to happen.

"Yup." Turning, she cups a hand beside her mouth and yells, "Stefano! J's staying for snacks." Then she turns back to me. "There, now you have to stay or Stefano will be upset that you didn't eat what he's preparing for you. Come on." Moving away from the door, she heads in the same direction Polo disappeared in, fully expecting me to follow.

Stefano is the house manager for the Mancini's. He's been with the New York mafia since pretty much the day he was born, working for Marco's father before him. His cooking is second to none and the way he cares for the family and those around them is amazing. Really, we're all his family, and he'd have it no other way.

Now, to refuse his food is not an option, because if I did, I know I'd be receiving tupperware boxes full of it on my doorstep. He's a persistent little Italian man, and one of only a few that I actually pay attention to.

The kitchen is huge, exactly how Stefano likes it. It's fit to feed an army of people with the amount of counter space and gadgets in here, and every single thing is put to use at some point.

I head to the breakfast bar, sitting on the stool River has clearly pulled out for me next to her, and wrap my hands around the fresh coffee already in front of me.

"Where's Stefano?" He's not in here with us, and now I'm suspicious.

"Whoops? He's out shopping, so snacks from the fridge it is. I've been so hungry lately, there's always a healthy supply of pastries." River shrugs, a low smile tugging at the corners of her mouth, knowing full well she just tricked me into staying.

"Devil woman." If it was anyone else, I'd be letting them see the tip of one of my blades through their fucking eye socket. But this is River, my boss's wife, the queen of the New York mafia, and while she may not be skilled in the killing department, she's a bad ass bitch that I respect the fuck out of.

"What can I say? You've taught me well." She laughs, nudging my shoulder gently. "Now tell me what's going on in that head of yours. Woman to woman, no bullshit."

"There's no—"

"J." That's all she says, interrupting me as it was obvious I was about to omit my truths. Her stare is hard but kind, and she doesn't push any further, just sits there patiently waiting.

The scent of fresh coffee fills my senses as I inhale, long and deep, exhaling sharply and shaking my head.

"I have a daughter and her father is my childhood sweetheart. God, that sounds so fucking sappy. But there ya go, in a nutshell." River's eyes widen as I explain, telling her as little as I can about my past and letting her in on what's been going on. She doesn't try to interrupt; even when I take a long pause to sip my coffee or gather my thoughts—which are all over the place—she remains present, listening intently.

"Okay, so my first thought is that you're being a bit of a dick. Actually, no, first... you have a daughter! That is absolutely the last thing I ever expected to hear come out of your mouth, but honestly, I think you'll be a great mother." She pushes her short dark hair back from her face. "But wow. And yeah, you need to pull your head outta your ass." Standing, River moves to grab the coffee pot and pours us both another, the first one long gone.

As I've said before, if she were anyone else... knives, blood, all the things. But I know she's not trying to be horrible or make me feel bad, she just doesn't hide behind pretty words when they're not needed. She's always straight and to the point, never afraid to voice her opinion, even in the face of dangerous people.

"I know. But he doesn't know that the Irish mob still wants to kill me. He doesn't know that I took the money and weapons my parents stole from them. They've looked after him and Hallie, given him opportunities, and if I stick around I'm gonna fuck it all up for them. Upend their lives. All because I want a happily ever after for myself. How selfish is that?" The coffee's still hot, the steam heating my cheeks as I sip at my fresh drink.

"How selfish is it for you to hold yourself at arm's length from them? Giving them only small glimpses of what might've been then taking it all away because you're scared. You, J, *scared*. Doesn't sound right, does it?" Fucking woman's full of all kinds of wisdom, like anything's possible, and while our worlds may be connected, my world isn't hers. It's not as simple as all that.

It can't be.

"But the Irish—"

"Fuck the Irish. You found a way out once before, you can do it for your family. And this time, you've got an army by your side."

The conversation with River was enlightening, to say the least. Never did I believe she'd be able to school me, of all people, in being tough, but fuck me, she did it.

Nobody scares me, and I've allowed the thought of family to push me back thirteen years into the scared little girl I once was instead of letting it make me stronger.

After riding home to grab a change of clothes, I'm now at the casino, where I've been watching Mr. Wright play Blackjack for the last hour. My mind may be whirling with questions about my personal life, but business is business. I need to separate the two or I'm fucked.

My phone vibrates in my pants pocket—black like my soul—and I dig it out from my corner of the casino. I do love to play, but my main focus tonight is following Mr. Wright's every move.

Unknown: They've found you

What the actual fuck?

Me: Who are you?

I wait for ten, fifteen, minutes, and no reply. My jaw aches from grinding my teeth as I try to figure out who "they" are, my mind going at a million miles a minute when I notice Zavier making a beeline for me.

I was hoping to avoid him tonight. His fascination with me is annoying.

"Ah, Shadow. Nice to see you again. You not playing tonight?" Zavier sits beside me at the small corner bar, following my eyeline to Mr. Wright. "Got your eye on something else, I see..." He rests his arm on the back of my chair, his fingers brushing against the leather of my jacket as he leans in to tickle his breath across the skin of my neck.

I don't flinch, don't move, allowing him to feel like he has some power here. Even though we both know he has none.

Hopefully my silence also tells him to back off. I'm not in the mood to play flirtatious with him tonight.

It's then that Mr. Wright chooses to up and leave, having won a few big pots, yet again. I finish off my water, turning away from Zavier and placing the now-empty glass on the bar behind me before standing.

"Time for me to go." I don't waste time with pleasantries, taking the time to zip up my jacket as I watch Mr. Wright cashing in his chips from the corner of my eye.

"Stay, keep me company tonight, Shadow. I'm bored." His hazel eyes bore into me, pleading, but he's full of shit. He doesn't want me to follow the tall thin man I clashed with last week, the man he defended and very obviously has some kind of deal with.

"Only boring people get bored, Z." Without giving him a chance to reply, I head on outside to my bike and find a spot nearby so I can see the exit, ready to try my hand at tailing this guy. Shoo's the best we have for these jobs, so the fact Mr. Wright managed to lose him every time says this man is dangerous.

Everyone's considered dangerous until I know all their secrets.

Glitch has eyes on the internal cameras and his message telling me our mark is finally leaving the building comes through just as the door opens. Who I'm assuming is his bodyguard walks through first, a huge gorilla of a man, and hairy enough to be one too. The bodyguard is with him every time we've seen him, laying more suspicion on this creepy thin man, because who needs a bodyguard?

They get into a waiting black sedan idling by the curb, and it quickly moves off once they're inside. I wait a few moments before following behind so the rumble of my engine doesn't let them know I'm here, my headlight off too. We're on the outskirts of the city and I could outride any police if they caught sight of me.

So far, so good. We've been on the road for about twenty-five minutes and I'm still tailing behind the vehicle. The direction we're headed doesn't give away a final location, but I make note of the road signs I see anyway, a warmth spreading through my chest when I see one for Newark.

The sedan turns left up ahead onto what I know is Ferry Street and I'm curious to know where they're going. It's now one o'clock in the morning, so there aren't many other vehicles around, especially where we're entering a quieter area. This isn't exactly the best thing for me, my bike isn't exactly quiet, meaning I have to fall a little further back to avoid being seen or heard.

"Fuck!"

A sharp burning pain shoots into my upper arm, causing me to swerve right then left. No doubt in my mind I've just been fucking shot. I don't chance a look down, but considering I can still move it and it doesn't feel like blood is pouring out of me, I'd say it's more of a graze. Still fucking hurts.

I notch my bike down a gear and speed up, trying to catch sight of whoever was brave enough to shoot at me. There's a car I hadn't noticed a little ways behind me, also with the headlights off so I can't make anything out other than it's dark. *Fuck.*

Taking the same turn as Mr. Wright's sedan, I speed up some more. The other car follows.

I see movement through my mirrors, then a ping sounds off my bike, and another, until the fuckers take my back tire out and send me flying from my baby as it skids out. My body scrapes along the ground, pain pulsing through my hip, my knee, my already injured shoulder. And thank fuck for my helmet because my head smacks the road, bouncing up again and making my head throb.

The car engine gets louder, speeding up to catch me, and I'm in no state to try and take on whoever this is right now. I am, however, going to fucking run. Pain be damned. I won't give them the satisfaction of killing me. I'm not dying today.

With great effort, I manage to stand, removing my helmet and looking longingly at my smashed-up bike in the middle of the road before making my legs move as quickly as they can down a side street. The car screeches to a halt, I can hear the tires and shouts from at least four men trying to figure out where I am in the distance. One good thing about wearing all black, and just another reason I am the Shadow.

I keep moving, slower now. To where? I don't know. I'm going on autopilot because my phone got smashed in my pocket when I came off my bike. I can't call for my crew, I can't call Marco, I'm fucking screwed out here and beginning to wane, every muscle in my body aching with each movement forward. I think I've lost whoever the fuck it was that shot at me, and if I was in better shape I might've tried to stick around and spy a little, but I know how to survive. And sticking around was not an option.

I don't know how long I've been walking, but my eyes light up when I recognize the house now in front of me. The white picket fence, the winding path to the front porch steps, the truck in the driveway...

Two steps away from the door, my energy levels drop considerably and I know this is a mistake. I promised myself I'd keep them away from all of this, but I have no other option.

I manage to knock gently on the door before slumping down against it, not wanting to be too loud in case I wake Hallie. She doesn't need to see me like this.

Tapping gently again, I decide it's probably for the best if Murph doesn't answer the door. I'll just close my eyes for a few minutes, get my energy levels back up again, then find a way home.

But why does it feel like I'm already home?

CHAPTER FIFTEEN
MURPHY

She left a note. A fucking *note*.

Actually, no. She left a piece of paper with one word on it. "Sorry."

And what exactly is she sorry about? The orgasms? The undeniable chemistry and connection we felt? It wasn't in my head, either. I saw it in the way her eyes never looked away from me. The way her body shook with my touch. The way she let herself completely go, knowing she was safe in my arms.

The problem isn't us because the "us" of last night was utter perfection. No, the problem is altogether different and it has nothing to do with me and everything to do with her baser instincts. To be fair, I can't say I know Jordyn, not anymore, but some things don't change. Obviously.

As long as I can remember, Jordyn has been like a wild animal; raw and honest. Mostly, when she's backed into a corner, she only has two modes: fight or flight. Last night?

She fled as far as she could go, forgetting that the thing she's running from is the thing that's deeply embedded in her veins. Us. Hallie and me. Her only living family.

So, when I hear the faint knock on the door, I know. My Jaybear is back and I'm not sure how to deal with it. So I hesitate. I freeze at the kitchen door and bury my hands in my hair, wondering if this is worth it. If her disappearing acts are going to destroy my favorite girl in the world. My whole fucking heart. Before I even reach out for the doorknob, I have to consider the damage she's capable of inflicting on our daughter.

I will do anything for J, but I won't let her do that. Hurting Hallie is not an option, I don't care who the fuck it is.

On the flip side, though, keeping J from Hallie would be equally devastating and I can't live with myself if I were responsible for that. So I make a choice that I can live with... hoping that if or when J bolts, Hallie will run to me and I will shelter her from the pain.

Always.

With all my bravado and the ultimatums I'm practicing in my mind, I'm just not prepared for the sight in front of me as I swing open the back door.

"What the fuck?!"

J is sprawled over my stoop, her head lolling to the side as it follows the movement of the opening door. When our eyes meet, every conflicting thought I had minutes before just fly away and my only concern now is her.

As I reach out to help her up, she slaps my hand away, but it's faint, barely hitting its mark. With eyes unfocused and movements slow and sloppy, I can't figure out if she's drunk or hurt. But then she pushes herself up and I see it.

Her leathers are torn up, blood and flesh staining her black clothes. She's oozing blood from just above her wrist and the way she clutches her ribs with every effort she makes, I don't need to be a doctor to know she's, at the very least, bruised a rib, if not broken it completely.

"Jesus fucking Christ, Jordyn. For once in your life, just let me help you." I use her full name to get her attention and, in a move that I did not expect, she slumps in my arms and lets me pick her up to take her to the half bath near the kitchen. I don't want Hallie to walk down for a glass of water and find her mother half passed out and bleeding all over our kitchen. This way, I have a minute to shield her.

Sitting her down on the toilet, I wrestle with my drawers, one of them deciding today is a good day to get the rack stuck. Cursing from between my teeth, I let out a breath as the drawer finally opens and I can access the alcohol and hydrogen peroxide. I hand her the gauze for her arm, and without telling her anything, she knows she needs to stop the bleeding on her arm. It's when I reach for the cotton that I hear her speak but I'm so focused on my task that I don't understand her at first.

"I will fucking cut you if you use alcohol or that other shit on me. Water and soap. That's it." I'm no doctor, and this is not a hill I'd ever choose to die on, so I just shrug and grab a clean washcloth that I run under mildly hot water for a while, adding soap then lathering it up to clean the wound.

But when I actually see the wound on her side, I realize she's got tiny rocks and shit inside.

"Change of plans. You need to get into the shower and wash that shit away before you get it infected." She snarls a little, again, the wild animal in her making a predictable appearance.

"Take..." she stops after her first word, like she needs to concentrate on taking in another breath before starting over. "Take off my boots and pants. I can't move. I can't... breathe."

I swear to fuck, as soon as all of this is cleaned up, I'm going to need answers.

Carefully and with slow, measured moves, I peel off her leather jacket, trying my best to spare her more pain than what she's feeling right now. With every pull and tuck, she stiffens and grunts, never once complaining. But I know. Her pain is visible in the strain in her eyes and the white knuckles of both her hands as she tries to stay standing.

It wasn't a beating, that's for sure. I'm guessing she crashed her fucking death trap on wheels.

"Guess it's time to buy a Volvo, huh?" The glare she aims at me could make grown men kneel and beg for mercy. Me? I chuckle. She's so predictable. "What? You gonna tell me you didn't crash your bike?"

"Later. Shower." I don't argue with her because she's right. I need to clean the wounds and make sure to give her some ibuprofen for the pain and the bruising I can already see forming just below the swell of her breast.

"Later is damn right."

At first, I thought I'd carry her, but as soon as I tried to pick her up, she flinched. Clearly, walking is going to be easier. I hold her steady by the waist, my skin against her skin, my fingers just above her hip keeping her upright.

"You okay, Jaybear?" I whisper my question as we pass by Hallie's room, trying my best to make as little noise as possible. It's a school night and I can't bring this kind of stress to my kid.

"Yeah, I'll be dandy." Sarcasm, it's her M.O., I'm learning. It didn't used to be so much. Yeah, she was always different, always sharp with her wit. Observant, too. When we were kids, we were sure we'd become cops. Fighting the good fight, putting away the bad people and saving the innocents.

Now look at us.

I have no idea what she does but I can guarantee it's not law enforcement. Although, I wouldn't put it past her to be an enforcer of some kind.

Once we're in my master suite, I undress down to my boxers, hesitating for a second before taking those off, too. It seems ridiculous to wear them after what we shared last night. We're well past that.

"Do you want me to take off your bra and panties?"

"I can do it." As soon as she bends at the waist, her knees buckle from what I'm guessing is the sharp pain at her side, right where that bruise is getting darker and darker. "Fuck."

"Alright, that's enough. You've played your hard ass, didn't cry or beg for help. I get it, J. You're the toughest person I know, but right now? I'm here, and I'm telling

you... I'm going to help you and you're going to let me."
If her eyes rolled any higher she'd be counting the satellites
up in the sky.

As I slide her panties down her legs, I place my lips just
above her belly button and thank God she was wearing her
riding clothes and her helmet. I don't know how bad her
fall was, but if this is what she looks like with her equipment on, I don't want to imagine what happens without
it.

The contact of my mouth against her cold skin makes
her shiver and I'm hoping it's the good kind. She knows
she's safe with me, in all aspects of her life, but Jordyn has
lost too much to be fully trustful of anyone.

Once we're both in the shower, I make sure to do a thorough wash of her, from head to toe. With gentle fingers, I
lather her up, caressing her as I massage what I'm sure are
achy muscles. When I kneel at her feet and look up at her,
I see the spark in her eyes, the want, the need. I know it's
reflected right back in mine but this is neither the time nor
the place. Well, it could definitely be the place just not right
now.

"Make me feel good?" Steadying herself against the tile
walls, she buries her nimble fingers in my hair and pulls me
closer to her pussy, all wet and spread open for the taking.

I know what she wants… she wants a distraction from the throbbing in her side, but when I fuck her or make her orgasm, it'll be because she needs me, not as a substitute for daytime television.

Standing looks painful but I don't have a seat in here, it never occurred to me to install one.

"I'm almost done, Jaybear, hang in there." Her grunt is not in acknowledgement, it's in annoyance, and that simple fact makes me grin up at her. At this rate, she'll be back in love with me in no time.

I'm a patient man and she's the love of my life. What could possibly go wrong?

The next morning, I'm the one leaving her a note as I get up, get dressed, and take a completely unsuspecting Hallie to school on my way to work. As soon as we pull up, Hallie gives me a kiss on the cheek and pushes open the front passenger door, then pauses before turning back.

"You're letting all the cold air in, Hal." It's fucking freezing and that sky looks like it might dump a ton of snow on us at any time.

"Do you think Mom will want to live with us?" My immediate reaction is silence, my brain going back to this morning. Did she go into my bedroom? See Jordyn?

"Why do you ask that?"

"Hallie! Come on, we're gonna be late!" With a shrug, she bolts out of the car, throwing a, "See ya!" over her shoulder as she runs up to her friend—yes, they're friends again—Bridget. Ah, teenage friendships have more drama than the Kardashian sisters.

Her question stays with me all the way to the shop where I continue to think about it throughout the morning and well into the early afternoon. Close to half past one, Riley Callaghan struts in, his usual Wall Street Journal under his arm and a thick coat protecting him from the light dusting of snow outside.

"What's up, Murph? How's business?" Riley Callaghan is a name that means something around here. He and I grew up together back in the day. I don't remember a single day of my life without him. There are rumors that he's training to take over his father's business, but I don't get involved in that part of their shit. I crunch the numbers, make sure all the cars are looking good and legal, then do all the necessary paperwork for them to sell them back at double the price after minimal work on them... mostly aesthetics.

"It's all settled. That Beemer in the back is good to go but you may want to change the color. It's a pretty distinctive green, not a lot of them around here." Glancing up at the clock on the wall, I begin putting my things in order so I can go home, check on Jaybear, and eat a bite before picking Hallie up at school.

"We're moving it to Miami, it'll sell like fuckin' hotcakes there." He's not wrong but still... it's not an everyday color, but whatever. "By the way, heard a rumor about you."

I chuckle at this because our girls are constantly fictionalizing our lives with their dreams and expectations.

"Ah, you got word about my pancake making skills. Told you I could cook." I've got all my papers in my backpack and I'm about to walk out the door when his next words stop me dead in my tracks.

"Nah, I hear you've got fresh pussy at the ready. Even rides a bike?" Riley and I never talk about women here. This is our place of business and we've always kept our lives separate. I don't want my personal information bouncing off the walls of this place and I don't want the Irish information bouncing off the walls of my home. It was our deal and, for the last thirteen years, it's been held up.

I decide to shut this down because, for a reason I can't explain, I don't want to share the news about Jordyn just yet. Or ever. I know for a fact the Irish mob doesn't want anything to do with her. Their debts were settled when her parents paid the price with their lives. More even since she disappeared and Hallie was raised without a mother. Still, something just isn't sitting right with me. After all, he is the son of the man who ordered the hit.

"Ry, if I were seeing someone and you referred to her as 'pussy at the ready', I'd punch you in the fucking throat for your disrespect." I cock my head to the side to make sure he knows I'm not fucking joking around.

"Fair."

"Good."

His questions follow me all the way home. I think about it as I pull up onto the driveway, ponder the reason why he'd even be interested in who I'm fucking. He definitely never has been before. I wonder if it was an innocent thing because Bridget said something now that the girls are on again. Then, as I walk up the steps to my room, I berate myself, thinking my reaction was too visceral, giving me away like a bad poker player.

But the second I walk into my room, all thoughts of Riley are gone. Vanished.

A lot like Jordyn fucking O'Neill.

Gone. Again.

CHAPTER SIXTEEN

J

When I woke up surrounded by the scent of what can only be described as pure Murphy, I almost rolled over and went straight back to sleep. Only the pain shooting through my ribs reminded me what the fuck happened in the early hours of this morning.

The house was empty when I left Murphy's bedroom, dressed in one of his t-shirts and a pair of sweatpants I've had to roll at the waist so they stay up. I was so happy to find a landline phone hanging on the wall by the kitchen, immediately using it to call into my Reapers—I could hear Crank going batshit in the background when I told them what happened. He had spent a lot of time tuning my baby up and making sure it was exactly what I wanted, so to know it's been totaled is a bit of a kick in the gut for him too.

My next call was to River, because she and Marco are two of the only people I am willing to let into this other side of me. It was fucking stupid of me to come here last night, but River was right. I'm hurting them whether I stay or not, so why not allow myself a small piece of happiness?

I need to sort this shit out with whoever came for me last night and figure out if it has anything to do with why Mr. Wright is so damn difficult to tail. I thought I had it in the bag until the trigger-happy fucks turned up.

Once I've sorted my shit out, then I can do this; spend more time with Murphy, maybe try and be a real family with Hallie, maybe take on some less dangerous jobs...

A conversation with Marco is in order at some point. I know he'll be able to help.

Now, though, I'm in the passenger seat of Marco's classic red Aston, being driven to the Reapers' clubhouse by River. She's immaculately dressed, as usual, wearing a royal-blue, wide-leg pantsuit, her short hair styled. I explained what happened on the phone, so the journey back to New York from Jersey is silent, bar the beautiful growl of the V8 engine.

I left another note for Murph; not the same shitty "I'm sorry" that I left the other morning. Instead, I told him I'd see him in a couple of days and that I'd text him my new number as soon as I get a new phone.

Beside me, River sighs; a telling sign that she has something on her mind, and I know the silence is about to be broken.

"You decided what you're doing with them yet?" *Them* being Hallie and Murphy, I'm assuming. She doesn't take her eyes off the road, which I'm thankful for because it's frosty and threatening snow outside.

My response is a shrug. River's known me long enough to understand when I'm not in a talking mood, and now is one of those times. She doesn't need to be looking directly at me to know my answer.

"Okay, I get it. I will say this though, you think you've got problems? I took a pregnancy test this morning and it came back positive." She laughs, but it's a little awkward.

"How is that worse than getting shot at?" I could also go into detail about discovering that the little girl I thought died at birth is still alive, but we covered that yesterday afternoon. She knows. This is just River having a sharing moment. She does that sometimes.

"It just is. You gonna argue with a pregnant lady?"

Fucking hell, she's gonna be one of *those* pregnant women. I roll my eyes and just stare at the side of her head.

"Sorry. I didn't have a coffee before I left because I don't know if I'm even allowed coffee anymore, and I'm freaking out because my life is over without coffee." Her voice gets higher as she speaks, and I'm certain she's speeding up a little too.

"I mean, my life was almost *literally* over, but sure... coffee."

"Yeah, okay. Po-tay-to po-tah-to. You're lucky Marco even let me out of the house after you called. When I left, I think he was ordering the cage and bubble-wrap, ready to contain me for the next nine months."

Now I do laugh, because she's not wrong and the mental image of Marco being a father is something I'm actually looking forward to seeing.

"For your baby's sake, I hope it's not a girl or she won't see the light of day until she's at least thirty."

"He can try." She turns her head to me and smirks, slowing down the car as we near the Reapers' clubhouse.

"Thanks for the ride, Riv. I'll see you in nine months, I guess." Smiling, I give her a wink and climb out of the car.

Other people being pregnant, having babies, has never really given me any huge feelings. My own tragic experience with childbirth is something I've never wanted to put on someone else, so I have always pushed my negative thoughts on the subject down. Locked them away. And while the image of the quiet baby girl I thought had died will always haunt my memories, it doesn't mean I can't be happy for my friend.

To be honest, the fact that Hallie is alive and well has eased the dull ache that has permanently flowed through me for the last thirteen years.

With a rev of the engine, River drives off and I'm glad I thought to grab one of Murphy's hoodies to wear before leaving his house. Frost grips the leaves on nearby bushes and the chill in the air seeps into my aching bones.

I key in the code to the entrance and head inside the Reapers' building. There are loud voices coming from the kitchen, so I follow them, knowing exactly what I'm going to find. Fizz has set up a lunch spread across the large dining table where we often eat together during jobs. We're not always working on cleanup; Crank has his own garage, Shoo works in a tattoo studio, Tab owns a bar downtown, and Glitch is a web designer. Fizz and some of the others prefer to stick around the clubhouse when they're not at their own apartments, keeping things running around here and making sure we all always have what we need on hand.

Every Reaper is valuable.

And they're all here now. Completely ignoring me because they know I'd tell them all to fuck off if they made a fuss. It's kind of nice, how well they get me and I them. The last time we were all together like this was when we accepted Binx into our ranks a few years ago.

"Made you a plate." Fizz appears beside me, plate of food proudly in hand, and the pile of meat makes me smile.

"Thanks." I accept as graciously as I'm able. None of us will say it, but she did this for me so I don't get jostled as the others attack the food like starving men.

Fizz nods sharply, just the once, smiling before taking a seat at one end of the table while the others continue to fill their own plates. I follow, taking a seat beside her, and dig into my bacon and sausages.

Like this, it's easy to imagine Murphy and Hallie being a part of my world. The fun family time we spend together, laughing and joking. But I know as soon as we've finished eating, I'll be pulling some of them aside to find out what the fuck happened last night.

"Spare truck in the garage for ya, J. Came from a job about a year ago and it's just been sitting there. It's clean, so it's all yours until we sort you out a new ride." Crank continues to eat opposite me as he speaks, like he's just discussing the weather and not the fact that I'm devastated about losing my bike.

"Thanks. Speaking of, did anyone go out after I called to see if it'd been called in yet and check the damage?" I finish off my bacon and wash it down with the coffee that was conveniently placed in front of me when I sat down.

"Yeah, I took Binx with me in the van. There was no sign of anything. No marks on the road, no debris, no police warnings, and worst of all, no bike. Glitch is on it though. He's been doing what he can to hack into the CCTV in the area. Fizz made him come out for lunch though, so I dunno how far he's gotten." Crank scoops up the last of his eggs, shoveling them into his giant mouth before standing and taking his plate over to the dishwasher.

The hustle and bustle of cutlery on plates, raucous laughter, and a million conversations sounds through the kitchen, making me smile again. I find it so easy to drop my mask of indifference with these people.

When I see Glitch rising from his seat and cleaning up his dishes, I ruffle Fizz's hair and head to the ground-floor office, otherwise known as "Glitch's tech room, keep the fuck out".

He joins me a few minutes later, sliding onto the deep-blue high-backed swivel chair in front of the wall-length desk. There are several screens, keyboards, and a few other things I don't even care to figure out. This is Glitch's domain and we all generally leave him to it.

"What do we know?" I get comfortable on the blue two-seater sofa against the opposite wall to the desk, behind Glitch, and he spins to face me.

"We know someone took your bike from the side of the road about an hour after you came off it. Whoever it was is fucking good. There is literally no trace of the person. They knew all the angles to avoid showing their face or anything incriminating on the CCTV and the vehicle they were driving is registered to a woman who died a year ago, two states over." He takes a deep breath and I stay silent, waiting for him to continue because he's obviously not done. However, my fists are clenched tightly by my sides at the thought of some fucker in possession of my bike. "The shooters, though, weren't connected. They drove off to try and find you and never returned to the scene. I did get a hit on them. The owner of the car was Shane Brennan. They began tailing you within five minutes of you entering New Jersey."

Fuck.

I hate to jump to conclusions, but I knew of a Shane Brennan when I was younger. He was a good few years older than me and well known for being a merciless cunt.

He was also quickly moving up the ranks with the Irish mob.

Double fuck.

"Do we have an address?"

"Yeah, but, J... we'll need to clear this with Marco first because they're out of state. And..." He scratches the back of his head awkwardly.

"Spit it out."

"Well, fuck. It's just... I think we should discuss some things with the rest of the Reapers and I might need to know, because the Irish mob have put a hit out on you."

CHAPTER SEVENTEEN
MURPHY

"I don't give a fuck, ship it out!"

Riley throws the door open, deepening the indent from the door knob, and I can't help but sit back and raise a questioning brow at his antics. When he yells back over his shoulder at Petey then slams the door like this day couldn't possibly get any worse, I dart my eyes to the computer screen to check the time.

It's only nine in the morning so this is just a preview of the day that's ahead of us. By the time evening rolls around, he'll be stabbing his employees for not spit-shining the bumpers.

"Go easy on the kid, it's his first week." At seventeen, Petey is barely out of diapers as far as mechanics are concerned. A week into his first internship, he's already done an oil change on a nineteen-eighty-six Subaru but forgot to put the drain pan underneath. Then he rotated the tires on Riley's Beemer, who later crashed his car two miles out.

Turns out Petey here didn't check the lugs in the right front tire. The only reason the kid is still here is because he's Riley's nephew and his mother, Ashley, would chop Riley's balls off if he fired her little boy.

So, we're all suffering in silence.

"I almost fucking died because his mother babied him his entire fuckin' life." With dramatics that rival Hallie's teenage tantrums, Riley drops into his chair and pinches the bridge of his nose, not bothering to open his eyes as he speaks.

"Ain't the same generation, Ry. We were basically raised by wolves." I shrug, remembering how simple life was before I realized what world I was living in.

"Yeah, well, these kids, now, are like helpless bunnies and if Petey don't get his head out of the fuckin' clouds, he's gonna get eaten' up by those fuckin' wolves." Meaning, us. We're the wolves now, yet we're all afraid of the mother bear.

"Death would be better than dealing with your pissed off sister." We both grunt because truer words have never been spoken. Ash was the oldest of all us neighborhood kids by one year and she took her job very seriously. She once punched a kid in the nose for telling Riley he had buck teeth.

No one fucks with Ashley.

"Oh, I'm supposed to tell ya that Bridget wants to go to the movies tonight to see something about barbie dolls or some shit. Wanted to know if Hallie could go with. I'll take 'em and pick 'em up." Reaching for his coffee, he brings it to his mouth, his eyes on me and waiting for my answer.

It's not that I don't trust Riley—I do, he's like a brother to me—but the thought of Hallie in downtown Newark always makes me nervous. She's only thirteen, and not by a lot, so her sitting in a crowded theater with fuck knows who doesn't sit well with me.

She's all I got. She's my north and south and my east and west. No matter what direction I go in, she's the one guiding my decisions.

"Christ, Murph, it's not like they're goin' clubbin'. It's the damn movies with a bunch of other teens and preteens watching a flick about dolls. How bad could it be?" Ry pops two aspirin into his mouth and washes them down with his coffee, leaning back in his chair and closing his eyes like this entire conversation is doing him in.

"Fine. But you go in with them." My glare could melt the skin off him but he doesn't even flinch.

"I ain't watchin' a bunch of dolls prancin' around singing and dancin'. Fuck that shit. I'll get Ash to go. She's always whining about wanting a girl." Of course she is. She's got four boys, and from what I gather, she's giving up trying for another in fear of getting another boy that she'll have to chase around the yard.

I got news for her, it doesn't matter the gender, teens only listen to teens and that's the only real problem in this world.

"Fine, you fucker. But if she comes home asking me to redecorate her entire room, I'mma hold you responsible for that shit." I won't. If Hallie asks, I'd do it in a heartbeat with a fucking smile on my face the entire time.

"Right." And he knows it.

The rest of the morning we work in silence as he does his inventory, moving cars around, changing license plates, shipping out the sold cars and bringing in the newly acquired ones. Meanwhile, I'm crunching numbers to make sure we're on track, never inching too close to the red line but making sure our revenue stays within the margin of the possible with a business like ours.

As lunchtime rolls on by, I close my computer and pack up my shit.

"What time's the movie?" I ask him, just as Petey knocks then walks right in, interrupting Riley's answer.

My chuckle does not go unnoticed if the middle finger he throws at me is any indication.

"Hey, Uncle Ry. That bike you wanted me to ship is leaking oil. Should I get it fixed up before I pack her up?" I'm not looking at either of them as those words slam into my ears and short-circuit my brain for half a second. Pure instinct is the only reason I don't falter, my gestures as fluid as they were, like the mention of a bike mere days after Jordyn showed up half mangled doesn't send a jolt of fear running through my veins.

I need to get the fuck out of here and have a long fucking conversation with J, and it can't wait for her to feel comfortable about it.

"All right, see you guys on Monday." I grab my bag and almost make it to the door before Riley's voice stops me dead in my tracks.

"Murph."

Looking at him over my shoulder, I search his eyes for any malice, anything that would say he's got my girl's bike in his possession, eager to get rid of it. I'm bouncing from one eye to the other, making sure that he's not working with some asshole who possibly hurt my girl. Or worse... that he's directly responsible for her being shot. I really don't want to see that in his eyes. Not now, not ever.

"Seven."

I frown at his word because it makes no sense in my rampaging thoughts. "Tonight, man. Movie's at seven so I'll pick her up at six fifteen." To play the part of the clueless accountant that's only here to get the numbers right, I roll my eyes for good measure.

"I'll let her know. Thanks." With a short nod aimed at Ry, I pat Petey on the back as I squeeze through the door before casually walking out like I do every other fucking day of the week. Except, this time, I'm a mess inside. Thoughts of people trying to hurt J are running through my mind but nothing makes sense. I feel like the kid at an adult table listening to an encrypted conversation.

My only job is to keep Hallie safe, which means I'm gonna have to grow up real fucking fast so I can keep my promise to her the day I found her screaming on that bed.

"Shhh, baby girl, I got ya. I got ya. You're okay, now. I'm here and I won't let anyone hurt you, I promise."

When I get home, I follow my normal routine before my school run. Eat, tidy up the kitchen, laundry. It's insane the number of clothes Hallie wears in just a couple of days' time.

Stepping into her bathroom to grab the hamper, I roll my eyes at the sight in front of me. Shit is everywhere. Hair shit, makeup shit, towels on the floor, clothes hanging from the hamper like they're trying to save themselves from the doom of the washer.

It feels like negotiations are in order... *movies IF you clean your room*.

I read somewhere that the carrot is better than the stick. I've never laid a single hand on Hallie, never had to if I'm honest, so the carrot has been good to me for the past thirteen years.

The same book said that children and teens are two completely different children, so who the fuck knows? The only thing I can count on is that I love that kid more than life itself and I make sure she knows it every day. Anything beyond that is just fingers crossed.

As I'm putting the dirty clothes in the washer, I see Jordyn's note from a few days ago. I smile at the memory. It'd felt like a small victory, her writing to me—explaining, promising.

There's no denying that there are times our entire relationship is a give on my part and then... nothing. She doesn't necessarily take but she doesn't give much either. I don't know about the life she's been living these past thirteen years but I can't forget that her sixteen-year-old self was not spared from tragedy. It's impossible to imagine how she even survived that kind of trauma.

But this note was a step and I'm hanging on to that hope because it's the only thing I've got.

"I need a couple of days to sort shit out. I'll give you a call as soon as I get a new phone. Thanks, Murph."

This is her showing me she's trying to be with us, trying to include us in her decision making. Hell, I can practically see a little heart drawn right next to my name.

Shaking my head, I return to reality. The day she draws a heart on a note is the day I need to see a doctor for dementia.

Once my chores are done, I head over to my home office and click on the program that allows us to keep up with all of our vehicles at the garage. I need to know if this was her bike instead of making assumptions based on pure coincidence. The way I've set this up, every car is divided into make and model with a separate spreadsheet for bikes. For the last six months, we've also been working on scooters and electric bikes so they get their own spreadsheet as well.

The mechanics are supposed to keep track of the vehicles they work on and make sure they fill out this spreadsheet in due time so I can work my accounting magic in the background.

But when I pull up the bikes, there are no new entries. Nothing more recent than six days ago, which was a dirt bike that needed legit work for a competition upstate.

Logging out, I let my mind work on piecing what little information I have into something that makes an iota of sense. It could just be Petey, his head is in the clouds more often than a fighter pilot's.

Punching out of the system, I'm practically fuming with frustration, knowing every single fucking person around me is keeping shit from me. Normally, it's what I want when it comes to the garage. The less I know, the better. But this time it has to do with the safety of my daughter and I'm not okay with that.

What's pissing me off the most is that, as of this very second, I can't do a fucking thing about it. I've got no way of reaching J, and talking to Riley about it would only make things worse. If I were to bring up the bike, he'd get suspicious since I never ask questions when it comes to his side of the business. Not to mention, I have no fucking clue if all of this is even an issue. There are a million bikes in the tri-state area. Petey could have been talking about any number of them. Regardless, no one—not a single fucking soul—wants to see Riley suspicious or worse... angry.

It's almost three when I grab my keys from the counter and head out. Hallie's going to be excited about going to the movies and will probably need the three hours to get ready for the evening.

Just as I slide into my truck, the buzzing in my back pocket reminds me to slide my phone out so I don't crush it under my weight. Glancing at the screen, I see it's a text from an unknown number. I usually ignore these things when I'm in the car, but I can't help the feeling it's important.

As I unlock the screen with my thumbprint, the smile on my face pops the corners of my mouth up. I can't help it. It's her and, true to her word, she's giving me the means to contact her again.

This thing between us can work, I know it. We just need to communicate and hopefully her barriers will drop. Mine? Well, they've never really been up with her. Not ever. No matter how devastated I was when she disappeared, I knew in my heart and soul that if she were to show up at my doorstep, I'd forgive her in a heartbeat... no questions asked.

Turns out, I'm the one who found her, but she doesn't know that. It was a complete coincidence and, to be honest, I wasn't even sure it was her at first. As I sat in the corner booth at that mom-and-pop diner, I practiced all the things I wanted to say to her, watched her eat alone, sipping on coffee all day long just staring out the window like she was contemplating the meaning of life, wondered what she was saying in the letter it took her two hours to write and who she was writing it to. At first, I was pissed... livid, even. How dare she have the luxury of time to sit all fucking day while I was playing mom and dad at home to our daughter? The only reason I was even there was because my parents had taken Hallie to Florida on her eleventh birthday for a weekend in Orlando doing all the Disney things.

The next year, I went back to that diner, thinking... no, hoping... I'd been wrong. Rationalizing to myself that I'd hallucinated the whole thing. No way did I see Jordyn fucking O'Neill in some random diner looking like a badass dream.

Turns out, I wasn't wrong. My Jordyn came to this diner every year, like a parenthesis to her life. With hindsight, it's safe to say she was probably thinking about Hallie. Punishing herself for the mistakes she made as a teenager.

That's when my anger melted away and empathy grew instead.

That's why I told Hallie the minute she asked me if I knew.

It was time we all moved on from the punishment, time to heal from the past.

It's me. Here's my number.

Instinct makes me add her to my contacts under the name "Mama", as in baby-mama, but if anyone were to grab my phone or see it ring, they'd think it's my mother.

Me: *We need to talk, and soon.*

Mama: *Yeah.*

I swear, I need to teach her basic social skills.

Me: *Hallie is going to the movies with her friend Bridge. Come by after seven.*

Mama: *K.*

I decide in that moment that I'm going to fuck the one-word answers right out of her. Tonight.

CHAPTER EIGHTEEN

J

The people Murphy works for want to kill me. Two days ago, when I last came to New Jersey, they almost succeeded. Well, they tried anyway.

After all these years of staying off their radar, I've fucked up. I got too confident in my ability to do it all and allowed the thought of the family I never believed possible to cloud my judgment. Not that I'd have it any other way. Knowing Hallie and having Murphy back in my life are two things that I'll always treasure.

I just kinda wish I had been a bit more vigilant to begin with.

The thing is, they have a life here, and Hallie has friends; persuading them to move to New York because it's safer for them is gonna be a feat in itself. It may only be the next state over, but I have resources there, I have access to any number of things and people that can make sure my family isn't in harm's way like they are now. Which is absolutely my fault, but I'm trying to fix it.

Until the Irish mob problem is over, Marco—or more like River—has insisted that Murph, Hallie, and I move in with them in their huge mansion of a building opposite Central Park. While that wouldn't be my first option, it's the best one I have, and I've been assured that we'll still have our privacy for however long I need it.

When I finally let my Reapers in on what was going on, after we discovered the hit on me, Fizz and Shoo tried to persuade me to take Murph and Hal to the Reapers' clubhouse. I won't lie, I thought about it as an option, quickly ruling it out when Flower came back from a cleanup smelling like disinfectant with splashes of blood on her cheek. She had insisted on doing a cleanup job on her own after being away in Barbados with her girlfriend for the last three weeks, said she had missed the precision needed on a job like that.

All these thoughts are swirling around my head as I pull up in front of Murphy's house in the stupid truck from the Reapers' garage. It's big and clunky and nothing at all like the freedom of riding my bike, however, the truck is easier to navigate on the icy roads in this weather. Only a few more weeks and spring should finally be hitting us, but

I know I'm gonna be gutted about losing my bike all over again when the ice begins to thaw.

With a deep breath, I jump out of the truck and walk up the short path to Murphy's forest-green front door, my boots crunching the ice into the pavement. Before I have a chance to knock, the door is open and there stands a smiling Murphy dressed in my favorite outfit of his...

Absolutely fuck all.

His brown eyes bore into mine, his chestnut hair falling into his face, and he holds a hand out to grab mine, pulling me into him.

"Come here, Jaybear."

Everything I need to say to him flies out of my head, replaced by the need to get as naked as Murphy is as he devours my mouth. His tongue slides against mine, his hand grips my braided hair, and the door clicks closed behind us. Even when he grips me tightly, his touch is kind, gentle, and full of love. The hand not tangled in my hair is caressing my back, squeezing my ass, cupping my breast, moving everywhere he can reach without pause, and I moan into his mouth.

"Too many clothes." Lips still locked as best we can, we both attempt to undress me as quickly as possible. He chuckles, his bare chest vibrating against my now-bare one, and I shudder at the contact as I toe my boots off and step out of my jeans.

The urgency in being naked and close to Murphy is like nothing else. He's intoxicating and I need to taste more than his mouth. Switching positions, I slam Murph back against the door and drop to my knees, my face now level with his thick, hard cock. I wrap my palm around the base, pumping slowly as I lick at his balls with the tip of my tongue.

The groan that escapes him is sexy as fuck, encouraging me to pump harder. His hands fist at my hair, fingers digging into my scalp as I suck the tip of his cock into my mouth, flicking at the end with my tongue.

"Fuck, J." His voice is a deep rumble, full of sex and lust, heating my core and making me pulse with need.

I move faster, taking him to the back of my throat until he pulls my head back, the sharp sting of pain in my hair setting me on fire for him.

"I need to be inside you." He tries to pull me up quickly but I raise an eyebrow, licking the tip of his cock again before slowly rising, brushing my chest up against him and slightly tilting my head up to meet his gaze.

"Come and get me." I wink before turning and taking measured steps toward the stairs, kneeling once I'm halfway up and pointing my ass in the air, my pussy on full show for him. Looking over my shoulder, I see him now standing at the bottom, his chest heaving, his eyes on mine as a grin takes over his face.

"You're fucking beautiful." Murph moves up the few steps to me, stopping when he's level with my pussy and groans before sucking my clit. "And you taste fucking delicious."

I push back onto his face when I feel two of his thick digits entering me, in and out, yet it's not enough. I rock against his mouth and fingers, chasing the orgasm that's so so close, making my whole body alight with flames. Then it hits and I yell out, "Yeessss!"

His light chuckle against my pussy vibrates through me, causing the aftershock of my orgasm to intensify and I shudder. "Fuuuuck."

Before I can get comfortable or move to make him chase me some more, his thick cock is nudging at my entrance. I don't give him a chance to enter me slowly, taking his sweet-ass time. Instead, I push back, hard and fast, causing us both to moan out loud. With no teenager in the house, I don't have to hold back my screams.

Murph digs his fingertips into my hips and I wince a little at the pain in my bruised ribs as I arch my back to take more of him.

Lifting my leg, Murphy flips me over, a step now digging into my back as he continues to pound into me, hard and fast and desperate. He bends his neck and sucks one of my nipples into his mouth, biting at the end of it before bringing his face back to mine and doing the same thing to my bottom lip. We're all teeth and tongues and roaming hands as another orgasm rips through me. Murphy continues to fuck me through the aftershocks, another big *O* quickly building when he brings a hand between us and pushes his thumb against my clit.

The pain from the step against my back combined with my healing injuries from the other night are all aiding in making my orgasm stronger. Pain doesn't scare me, it excites me.

"Harder. Fuck, yes!" My words are breathy pants, but I need more, I need it all.

His thrusts become erratic and I know he's close, his grunts and groans getting louder with my own. I feel my eyes roll into the back of my head as another orgasm shoots through every inch of me and I scream out, Murphy quickly joining me with a shout of his own as he thrusts hard once, twice, three times before he stills.

We're both breathing heavily, our sweaty foreheads pressed together as we take each other in.

I shift slightly, needing to move, wincing again at the pain in my side as I sit forward and he moves back.

"Fuck, sorry. Did I hurt you, Jaybear?" The heat in his gaze turns to concern and his eyes scan the length of me. The graze on my shoulder, the bruise along my ribs, and a combination of both across my hip and thigh, all visible and things that someone else would cry over. But for me, they're just war wounds I'd rather have than being dead. I'm grateful for every scar, bruise, and cut I've ever had because they mean I'm alive and able to enjoy this moment with Murphy.

I smile at him, shaking my head. "No, Murph. I'm good."

He mirrors my action, letting out a huff of a laugh as he stands to his full height and holds a hand out for me to take. I'm eye level with his thick cock again, which looks about ready to go once more, but instead of tasting him, I kiss the tip and take his offered palm.

I know we need to talk, to figure out how to make this all work, but for now, I'm content to just enjoy this beautiful man who adores all of me with everything he has to offer that isn't reserved for our daughter. This man who has grown into everything he promised he would when we were kids, who fathered my child, who gives the best orgasms.

Orgasms from randos and while on jobs just aren't the same as this gorgeous man leading me back down the stairs and into the kitchen. I want to run again, to play with him, to experience the thrill of being with him in all the ways, but I can also smell something delicious coming from the oven. I'm torn between offering myself up with my legs spread wide or demanding a piece of the lasagna Murph's now pulling out and placing on the countertop.

"Thought you'd need to be fed more than just my cock." He winks as he washes his hands in the sink then grabs a knife and slices through the lasagna before pulling out two plates, serving a piece up onto each.

He's still completely naked and I have to laugh. "What if all I want is your cock? Hmm?"

Murph spins to face me, knife in hand, and I swear my pussy is begging to get some action at the thought of him bringing it closer to my own naked skin. "Then you'll be disappointed, Jaybear. Sit." He gestures to one of the stools and places a plate in front of me. "Eat."

Shrugging, I sit, the stool cool against my naked ass, and I inhale the deliciousness that is his cooking. Smells just like the way my mom used to make it.

"Don't have to tell me twice." I love food almost as much as I love orgasms.

His gentle smile warms my insides as he sits beside me with his own plate, stabbing some lasagna onto his fork and holding it up to my lips.

Okay, so I see how this is going to go...

I open wide, slowly closing my lips around the fork and sliding the food off into my mouth. Eating has never been so fucking hot, our naked bodies so close yet so far from the other. Then I take a forkful from my own plate and offer it up to him, our gazes connected the entire time. It's quiet and intimate and we take our time, the occasional nipple tweak or breast squeeze making sure my stool will be soaked by the time I stand up.

The dull vibrations of a phone going off ruin the moment and Murph rolls his eyes, leaning forward and kissing me so softly before standing and reaching for his cell. It's by the oven and at a constant state of buzzing at this point.

"That'll probably be Hal. No one else calls me at this time of night... well, except you now." He smirks at me as he lifts his phone to answer it without really looking at the screen.

At the same time, the shrill alarm of my cell catches my attention from the hall by the front door—where I stripped before getting thoroughly fucked. Standing from the stool, I leave the kitchen to go and grab my new phone, annoyed that I didn't have the foresight to turn the volume down, but also knowing that I'd never do that because I'm literally always on call.

I pull my cell from my jeans pocket and pause when I see the message flashing there from "unknown" again.

Unknown: They have her.

My heart sinks into my stomach and I think I might be sick, but I refuse to allow myself to jump to conclusions. That is until I hear Murphy's cry of desperation as he yells, "No!"

My hands shake with adrenaline and fear as I type a reply.

Me: If you touch a hair on her head, I'll scalp you myself.

The reply is almost instant.

Unknown: Not me. They. I'll text you if I get a hit.

Who the fuck is this joker? Does that mean they're helping?

I don't have time to try and figure it out as Murphy storms out of the kitchen, running straight for me, gripping the tops of my arms, his eyes wide with fear.

"She's fucking gone, J. What did you do?"

Chapter Nineteen
Murphy

"*She's fucking gone, J. What did you do?*"

It's every parent's worst nightmare. The late-night phone call. The guilt in the caller's voice. The confusion between what's real and what's impossible.

Fucking impossible.

How did this happen?

Ashley was there with them. Why was Hallie taken but not Bridget?

My brain hasn't reached the why part of the equation yet, I'm still struggling with the how and where.

How the fuck did this happen? And more importantly, where the fuck is she?

With a low, unsteady voice filled to the brim with venom, I made damn sure Riley understood that I expected every-fucking-one to work on getting her back.

"*We'll find her, Murph, I promise. We just need to know who did it.*" Those are the words running on repeat in my brain when I snatch up my scattered clothes and snap them on like they've personally offended me. It's the never-ending loop of *whodiditwhodiditwhodidit* ringing in my ears that prompts my accusation in Jordyn's face.

In this state of mind, where calm is nowhere to be found, she's the common denominator. As boring and mundane as our lives were living here in this home we built for ourselves, at least we were safe and happy. It's barely been three weeks since I gave Hallie permission to seek out her mother and, in that time, our entire existence has gone up in fucking flames.

"Murph, I need you to take a breath and tell me everything you just heard on that phone call." My eyes snap up to hers as I'm buckling my belt, wondering if she's lost her fucking mind.

"Did you just tell me to calm down?" My voice has never sounded deadlier. Not by a long shot.

"No, of course not." J's dressing at a rate I didn't think possible, almost fully ready to bolt. "But instead of blaming me, tell me what you know so I can get my resources out there looking for her." I scoff at her words. Resources? What the fuck resources does she have? I've got the fucking Irish mob on my side. What does she have? A biker gang?

"I'll handle it, J. I've got my own goddamn *resources*." That last word comes out mockingly, like I don't believe her. Truth is, I do believe she probably has people who could be out there looking but I'm too fucking angry and scared and hurt and fucking desperate to be logical.

My God, Hallie must be scared out of her mind. She's never even liked horror movies, they give her nightmares for days at a time. She is kind and loving and so fucking sweet. I can't lose her. Worse, I can't fathom someone hurting her beyond repair. Mentally or physically.

No. I can't think like this.

I'm grabbing my keys and am about to walk out the door when her next words stop me dead in my tracks.

"I work for Mancini."

The entire Earth feels like it's come to a complete halt, my brain struggling to catch up to this revelation. When I turn back to her, she's standing with her hands on her hips and her head hanging low, only her eyes are lifted and searching mine for a reaction. It's impressive how she's able to look guilty and unrepentant all at the same time.

When I don't respond, she continues. "That's who I ran to the night..." Clearing her throat, she looks up at the ceiling and takes in a deep breath. "I've been there this whole time."

Pieces of information are popping into place on this puzzle that I've never been able to put together. Hell, I still don't know jack about shit but this is...

Stepping inside, I slam the door shut and stalk her until we're nose to nose; me staring down at her with all the mingled emotions of a father needing to save his baby. "You get those motherfuckers on the streets, right now. Hell, you look closely to make sure they're not the ones responsible." I don't miss her recoil at my words, I'm sure she's going to...

"No. Fuck, no. Why the fuck would they take Hallie?" There it is. The denial.

"It doesn't take a fucking genius, Jordyn. That Italian prick and the Irish haven't exactly seen eye to eye in the last twenty years, have they? Now, you're back and they want leverage." It all seems so simple, why can't she see that? Italians are only loyal to Italians. They'll take any opportunity to get whatever they want, it's the way it's always been. It's why they fucking own all five boroughs.

"You don't know what the fuck you're talking about, Murph." Suddenly, she's calm, not a drop of panic in her voice like she just switched off all emotions. Texting to someone, she's not even looking at me. "What I need is where she was, exactly, who she was with, and what time she was taken."

"J, I'll…" I don't know how it fucking happens but I'm pinned to the wall with her hand at my throat and her teeth bared like a fucking crazed animal. If it weren't for the current situation, I'd stop and analyze why this position has me hard as a fucking rock.

"Don't. Now isn't the time to play *Gangs of New York*. We're going to find Hallie and we're going to get to the bottom of this fucking mess, but I need this information and I need it right fucking now, Murph. *Now*." Her words, combined with her aggressive approach, clear the haze of fog just enough for me to remember what's most important.

Hallie.

My fingers wrap around her wrist, squeezing for her to let go. Her hold was more of a warning than actual intent on hurting me but still, I need to be able to speak.

"She was at the downtown theater with Bridget. Her aunt Ashley was there sitting with them. About the middle of the movie, Hallie goes to the bathroom and doesn't come back." Those last words stay stuck in my throat, making me choke on them. "Movie started at seven so around eight something."

J's not even looking at me, she's texting every word I say to her so when I finish, she looks up at me, tenderness swimming in her eyes for the first time since I fed her lasagna.

"I have the best—the absolute best—on this." Then she does the most unpredictable thing she's ever done around me. She kisses the fear right out of me and, for a fraction of a second, I believe her. I believe without a doubt that she's going to do every fucking thing to find our daughter.

Pulling away, I cup her cheeks in my palms, my face close enough to kiss her again.

"I'm meeting Ry downtown. He said the police don't need to get involved, only the guys they've got on payroll."

J snorts and shakes her head. "Of fucking course," is her only answer as she pulls away from my hold and grabs her keys from the pocket of her leather jacket.

"What the fuck is that supposed to mean?" We're outside now, each walking fast to our own trucks when she turns, walking backward with her palms in the air like I'm the dumbest person in the fucking world.

"Doesn't take a genius to figure out who shot at me, Murphy!" Without giving me time to respond, she turns back around and jumps into her truck, pulling out with screeching tires and a fully revved engine.

I do the same but head in the opposite direction.

The whole ride over I've got a million things running through my mind. I'm shaking with adrenaline, my hands white with the steel grip I've got on the wheel and my heart breaking with every minute I don't get a call saying she's safe. All a big misunderstanding.

I park in front of a fire hydrant, not giving two shits if my truck is towed, yet knowing in the back of my mind that the last thing I need is to find myself without a fucking vehicle. Jumping out and slamming my door shut, I run up to Ry, who's standing just outside the entrance of the theater. Next to him, Ashley has her arms around a sobbing Bridget, patting her back and fighting back her own tears.

To say Riley is frantic is an understatement. I can see it in the way his teeth are clenched and his nostrils are flaring that he passed the pissed off level quite a while ago. Hallie and Bridget are like sisters. They fight as much as they love but they always come back to each other. It doesn't take a genius to understand that this happened on his watch—his sister being there was his idea—and he's dripping in guilt.

"Any news?" I don't bother saying hello. Who the fuck cares about being polite in times like these?

"We're getting eyes on the cameras," he tells me quickly in between screaming at whoever is on the other line.

"I'm so sorry, Uncle Murph. I'm so sorry." Bridget launches herself at me, her arms wrapped around my waist, squeezing hard as she rests her cheek on my chest.

"Hey, hey. This is not your fault. Do you hear me?" I squeeze her back as her father continues threatening people's lives on the phone. His growls and grunts reassure me. It's my proof that J's wrong. This wasn't the Irish, no matter what she thinks. It can't be. Ry is deep in the mob and he would never, never, hurt Hallie, and no one would do this without his knowing. It's just not how it works... I don't think.

"I should have gone to the bathroom with her." Fuck. If anything happens to Hallie, Bridget will be destroyed... another victim of this senseless crime.

My eyes catch Riley's when the screaming stops and I'm taken aback by the hardness I see in his gaze.

"What? What happened?" My grip on Bridget tightens, heart racing out of control once more just as three cops walk up to us. Now they're all staring at me like I'm the one who kidnapped my own fucking daughter. "What? Just fucking spit it out!"

"What the fuck was Jordyn fucking O'Neill doing at your house, Murph?"

The man in front of me isn't my best friend.

The man in front of me is the son of the head of the Irish mob.

He's lethal, he's pissed, and his venom is aimed straight at me.

CHAPTER TWENTY

J

"Who the fuck do you think shot at me, Murphy?"

I mean, come the fuck on. He can't be that dense on the whole thing, can he?

Without waiting for whatever excuse he's cooking up to defend his bosses, I turn on my heel and stride to my borrowed truck. My hands are shaking, my breaths are short, and I really shouldn't be driving in this worked up state, but I have no choice.

Murphy blaming me for Hallie's disappearance may have gutted me to my core, but he isn't completely wrong. I'm aware that me simply being around them was dangerous, and I was pushing my luck if I'm honest with myself.

This is my penance for leaving Hallie all those years ago. I should've checked her to be sure, but... fuck. This is a rabbit hole I don't want to be going down. Beating myself up about something I can't change isn't going to save my girl.

The look of pure devastation on Murphy's face, his cry of terror at the phone call; these are things that will haunt my nightmares, even after I've found her and brought her home safely. Because I *will* fucking bring her home safely.

"The light's fucking green, you fuckhead." I slam my palm against the horn, needing the vehicle in front of me to move out of my damn way.

It's raining heavily, the light from passing cars almost glowing off the droplets crashing against my windshield. Mixed with the snow from earlier in the week, there's no doubt black ice is on the road, but that doesn't stop me from wishing I had my bike right now so I could cut through this fucking traffic.

I need to try and rationalize my thoughts, which is usually something that comes so easily to me, but it's proving difficult in these fucked up circumstances.

For starters, who the fuck is the unknown number that's texted me more than once now? And how did they know Hallie was gone? Are they friend or foe? Because, at this point, they could be either. Glitch hasn't been able to get a trace on it at all yet, which is fucking weird.

Whoever it is, I can't wait to meet them face to face. Or maybe knife to face, right after I've slaughtered the fucknuts who have my daughter.

Terror and anger are warring inside me, each fighting for dominance within my veins, flowing through every inch of my body as I tightly grip the wheel. My knuckles are white, my muscles tense, and I barely remember one iota of my journey to the Reapers' clubhouse as I slowly pull to a stop out front.

Tab's already waiting for me by the entrance, arms folded across his giant chest. The group chat with my Reapers was my first point of call. I sent them all the information I have and they're already looking into what they can. They haven't asked for the specifics, but they knew something has been going on with me the last few weeks.

This is my made family though. I should've trusted them with everything before this point, and even though I didn't, they're still all hands on deck for me.

Rain continues to fall, soaking me as I step out of the truck and move toward Tab. The weather matches my dark and battered emotions.

Tab watches me, eyes full of concern, and he just nods as he steps aside for me to go into the house, following behind me and closing the door. Shoo appears as soon as we're inside, a large mug of coffee ready and waiting for me between his large palms.

I know it's mine because he'd rather drink a cup of shit than coffee.

"Where we at?" There's no time for pleasantries, not with the way this anger is flowing through the very fabric of my soul.

"The Irish cunts that Murphy works for have her. We know that much. What we don't know is *where* they have her. Yet." Shoo's quick rundown does little to reassure me.

"How the fuck do we know who has her and not where they've taken her?"

"After your accident, Glitch tracked the car that followed you with the shooters back to the Irish in Jersey, so Flower started tailing that fucknut, Riley. Mancini knows, I spoke to him while you were on your way here and got the go ahead to fuck shit up. We're done pussy footing around the Irish mob and it's time to clean house." Shoo looks pleased with himself, excitable even, at the thought of what we know we have to do.

"As great as that news is, you still haven't told me how we know they have Hallie." I'd like nothing more than to end the Irish fucks, but I need to be sure about this.

I may have gotten my revenge for my parents by killing the mob boss's two brothers years ago, but it wasn't exactly authorized by Marco's father, who was the Mafia boss at the time. The opportunity arose, I took it, then I asked for forgiveness after the fact. Of course, he understood and was even a little proud, and we all agreed to keep the mafia out of it so as not to cause a stupid gang war of any kind.

Having the mafia backing on this one will make things a hell of a lot easier, because with or without it, I plan on spilling a lot of blood for this.

"Riley was seen meeting with his dad, Ronan, just before seven, before they both headed straight for a bar near the movie theater you said the girls were at with a van full of their crew. When you texted, Flower called Glitch to run the plates on the van and was ready to change her target from Riley to whoever the fuck was in the van, but it'd already gone, nowhere to be seen. Only Riley was left and she watched him drive ten yards closer to the theater to begin playing the part of doting dad to his own kid. We discovered the plates on the van were fakes, and she's still tailing Riley as of right now." We've moved further into the house as he explains what we know so far.

"Okay, so we're working on assumptions rather than actual knowledge." I wouldn't say I'm angry with that, because my gut is telling me it was the damn Irish too, but concrete evidence is usually better to start a war with. Not that it'll be much of one because my Reapers and I are going to do the best cleanup we've ever done.

No fucking traces.

Shoo grimaces at my assessment of the situation. "Yeah." He shrugs.

I can't fault his honesty.

"We can work with that. Where is Flower now?" Wherever she is, Riley is, and that mother fucker is getting a visit from me very soon.

"Last we heard, he was seen arguing outside the movie theater before sending his kid home with the aunt. Flower's been following him for the last thirty minutes around Jersey and she's pretty sure he's figured out he has a tail. Either that or he's being real cautious because he's been circling." The whole time Shoo talks, Tab is standing stoically in the corner of the main living area, listening intently, ready to move out at a moment's notice.

"Where's everyone else?" I need to know who's on what and where so I can at least attempt to tackle this like any other situation we deal with.

"Fizz has been sent home, but she insisted we keep her up to date with what's going on. Crank basically forced her to leave after she had a panic attack. You know how she is when kids are involved, it's a big trigger for her. Crank's in the garage outside with Binx, fueling up some of the vehicles and checking everything's good to go." Gotta say, Crank doing this is always amazing. The one and only time he didn't, I got pulled over by the police because of a broken tail light, with a dead body in the trunk. Thank fuck it happened to be one of the cops Marco pays very well to keep quiet about what goes on in The City. "Glitch is in the computer room doing his thing if you wanna check in to see if we have anything new before heading out."

Nodding my thanks, I head for Glitch's work room, knocking once before entering.

He barely looks up from the computer screen to see who's come in. "Hey, Boss." He doesn't look like he belongs in front of a computer screen. In fact, he's great to have in the field when we need an extra hand, but this is his happy place. Despite his bulky, tattooed frame, he'd rather hide away than be out there in the real world. All of my Reapers have their own stories, their own tragedies and traumas, and that's just one reason we work so well together.

"Anything new to report, G?" I sit myself down on the small couch against the back wall, it's more of a perch, really.

"Kind of. I've got a trace on Riley's cell and I've been able to hack into it." Rubbing the back of his neck, he swivels in his chair to face me, the tap tap tapping of the keyboard now silenced. "According to his messages with his dad, they've had eyes on you for a couple of weeks. You keep disappearing on them, and this was their only option. They don't plan on hurting the girl, but they are trying to lure you into a trap so they can kill you. It seems that they don't know who you work for though, which gives us a little advantage. If they want to maintain the tentative peace, that is."

Everyone seems to be dancing around in circles with the information. It's all helpful, yet not even a little bit helpful. I'm frustrated as fuck with nobody to take all this rage out on.

"Your phone's buzzing like crazy." Glitch tilts his head toward my hand; I need to get ahold of myself and stay in the here and now, instead of imagining the Irish mob with heads on sticks.

Unknown: Fort Lee Soldier's Cabin.

My fingers are trembling at the information. It could be nothing, but it could also be everything.

"Can you trace this message?" Composing myself very fucking well, if I do say so myself, I hand Glitch my cell.

"I can try, J."

"Good, because whether it's a trap or not, the crew and I are heading over to Fort Lee."

Sitting around on my ass gathering information is making me feel about as productive as a wet napkin. The unknown texter has either handed me valuable information, or signed their own death warrant. Either way, I need to try.

My girl needs rescuing.

I just hope I don't lose what I've built with her dad in the process.

CHAPTER TWENTY-ONE

J

The hour-long drive to Fort Lee Soldier Cabin is monotonous and I didn't even take the time to appreciate the view as I crossed the George Washington Bridge. It's just after one in the morning now, but there are still more vehicles on the road than I'd like. Heading out of New York means we don't have the same protections when bending the law.

Shoo, Tab, and Binx are in the van behind me, loaded up with our cleanup tools—guns and knives included, because ridding the Earth of scum is in the same category as cleaning up. My black bomber jacket is perfect for concealing the harness full of daggers across my ribs, and the straps around my thighs and calves over my tight black pants hold just as many. Even my chunky ankle boots are loaded, and I have a gun on each hip. Gotta say, it's not super comfortable driving while this heavily armed, but comfort is the least of my priorities.

Flower texted just before we left to say she'd meet us there after some douche cut her off and made her lose the tail on Riley.

There's no road to the Fort Lee Soldier Cabin, it's part of a historical park site and in the middle of a copse of trees, like a mini forest. It's been closed down for about a year, so we're positive we won't have any other people to contend with. Which is something we're gonna have to hope luck is on our side for because CCTV around the area is non-existent.

I turn off the engine in the empty parking lot close to our destination, the van pulling in beside me, and I take in my surroundings once I'm out of the truck. The sky is dark, clouds rolling in, trees rustling as the wind whips through the branches, all of it adding to the somber mood that's fallen over me and my Reapers tonight.

Marco Mancini has rules, and leaving kids out of mafia business is a hard one. If this rule was broken, even our mafia family would have consequences. The fact that the fucking Irish mob deems it acceptable has just signed their death sentence.

"Load up, boys. Let's go see what kind of surprise is in store for us." My stomach is bubbling with a fear I wish I could erase, but I won't let those thoughts win out. I never do.

"Ready, Boss," is echoed from Shoo, Tab, and Binx as the grumble of a Mustang makes me look up. Flower has arrived, stepping out of her car as soon as it's parked and moving toward me.

"Sorry I lo—"

"Forget about it. Shit happens. We move on and find another way around it." My words are firm, but without malice, and she accepts every one like the badass she is.

"Okay." There's no argument from her, she just nods once and holds her fist out for a bump, knowing I'd probably stab her in the tit if she went for a hug.

"Let's go play!" Shoo is practically bouncing on his heels, waiting for us to begin our short trek to the cabin. Tab rolls his eyes, Binx shrugs, and Flower grins, excitement brimming through her veins.

Dead leaves rustle under our steps and I'm very aware that this could be a trap, but I'll never go down without fighting for my last breath. A trap is only a different word for showdown anyway.

With the cabin in view, the door just a few steps away, we're all a lot lighter on our feet—it still amazes me how Shoo and Tab could ever be considered as light-footed with their bulky weight, but they're fucking pros at this kinda thing. It's eerily quiet, the only sounds now are the light raindrops trickling through the trees.

I hold my palm up, signaling for my crew to stop where they are so we can assess our surroundings. Nothing.

Gesturing for them to silently surround the small wooden cabin, I place myself right outside the only entrance and take a deep breath. The windows are all boarded up, so there's no way to see inside. This is a total gamble and I'm ready.

I have a dagger in one hand and a gun in the other as I boot the door open—I might as well make an entrance.

Stilling in the doorway, I tilt my head in surprise, my eyes wide before a grin spreads across my face. What I find isn't what I was expecting, and I'm still mad as hell that it's not, but this will do to ease some tension. I whistle for my crew to join me, letting them know it's safe to come inside. This isn't a trap at all. It's a fucking torture chamber for Riley Callaghan.

He's hanging from a beam in the center of the room by his neck, a stool under his feet so he doesn't suffocate to death and a rope around his wrists. A beautiful black eye that brings me joy to see darkens his face and there's a gag in his mouth. As he eyes me, the old swagger I remember from years ago is trying to peek through.

"Well, well, well. What do we have here then?" Shoo laughs, circling Riley and flipping his own dagger between his fingers. "Boo!" he shouts in Riley's face, laughing harder when he flinches, almost losing balance on the stool.

I scoff, and as much as I'd love to stay and play, we need answers.

"Remove his gag, Shoo."

Using his knife, Shoo pokes at the gag, scratching Riley's cheek a little as the gag is roughly dragged from his mouth. Riley spits like the dirty bastard he is.

"Jordyn O'Neill. I wasn't sure if you were just a myth, ya know? Guess not." He laughs, a stuttered and breathless sound that tells me he's in need of water or a reprieve from the rope around his neck.

Flower is waiting outside, Tab stands in the entrance of the cabin, Binx moves to the far corner, and Shoo continues to circle Riley like a shark about to bite into his next meal. I take a step forward and rest a booted foot against the stool.

"Where the fuck is my daughter, Callaghan?" My tone is even, calm, nothing at all like how I'm really feeling inside.

"You mean the one you abandoned in a pool of her grandparents' blood?" He laughs again, a single syllable that makes me want to slice him up here and now.

"Yeah. The one that gave me the determination to get my own revenge by killing your uncles." I don't need to explain myself to him, the situation with why I left Hallie is none of his business, but I did feel the need to throw a dig back at him.

Watching his eyes widen in surprise is satisfying, but it's still not quenching my need for information.

"Where. Is. Hallie?" I say each word slowly, nudging the stool a little with each one.

"With her dad. Where else would she be? Do you really think I'd do anything to a girl who calls me uncle?" Just the sound of his voice is grating on my every nerve.

"Yeah, I do."

"Call him, see for yourself." His smug grin says he thinks he's one-upped me, so I call his bluff, sheathing my knife and pulling out my cell.

It rings a couple of times before Murph answers.

"Hey, Jordyn. Call off the search. She's with me."

Before I have a chance to speak, he's hung up, and I'm left feeling confused as well as angry. And why did he call me Jordyn?

"See? Told ya. Maybe take it as the hint Murph meant it as. You're dangerous. Stay away from them."

It all feels a little fucking off to me and I signal for Tab to take Binx for a perimeter check.

"You're a bit cocky for someone who's about to die, ya know." Shoo rests his chin on Riley's shoulder, making him wobble, off-balance with each word.

"You do know who I am, right? You'll never get away with killing me. The mob is already gunning for your head on a platter, girl. Fucking thieving scum is wha—"

The echo from my gun shot rings through the cabin, no doubt through the trees outside too. A circle of blood begins pooling from the wound in the center of his forehead and I kick the stool out from underneath him to let the bastard hang. I'd love to have spent more time here, but something still feels off about this whole thing.

Whoever the texter is did a fucking good job, and I'll shake their hand if I ever meet them, but this all feels like a wild goose chase to find my daughter who is apparently at home with her dad.

Riley's body makes some disgusting involuntary sounds as his body swings from the beam, blood dripping down his face and onto the floor beneath him.

"Good shot, Boss. I'll go get the gear."

This may be a closed down area, but we still need to clean up. We haven't been super vigilant up to this point, which will make this cleanup last a little longer, but it's what my crew does best.

"Get Binx in here to watch the place. I'll head back to the truck with you. I need to see her face before I believe this shit." I sigh heavily, waves of disappointment crashing through me at such an unsatisfying end for Riley Callaghan.

He deserved more pain than that, purely for being such a dick.

"Nothing to report, Boss." Tab heads over as I step outside.

"Okay. You and Binx stay here with Shoo to clean up. Text Crank, get him to head over to that Newark address I gave you. Flower will wait for him at the top of the street."

"On it." Tab nods and I turn to walk away, back to the truck.

Something's off with all this and I can't quite put my finger on what just yet.

What I do know is that by killing Riley Callaghan, I've already begun the war. And despite the fact that my daughter is safe in the arms of her dad, I won't leave something unfinished.

A relationship between me and Murphy, me and Hallie; they can only ever happen once the Irish have been eliminated from the picture.

As long as I'm their target, Murph and Hallie are in danger.

CHAPTER TWENTY-TWO

J

The entire drive back to Murphy's is a blur.

My emotions are rampant and my mind is racing back and forth from the most horrific hours of my life to what could potentially be even worse moments ahead. Having never gone to therapy, I don't know the extent of damage my parents' slaughter had on my mental health but it doesn't take a highly educated doctor to guess it's extensive. Enough so that, until this very inconvenient moment, I didn't have specific scenes flash in my mind.

13 years ago

"Sweetie, will you grab the plates for me, please? Your father is on his way home so we can eat at a reasonable hour."

Turning to the counter, I place my hands on either side of the stack of plates, and just as I lift them and turn, a spearing pain like nothing I've ever felt before shoots up my spine and across my entire swollen belly.

The plates fall, the sound of crashing ceramic against tile kitchen floors assaults my ears as I crouch to the floor and scream at the top of my lungs. My mother is immediately at my side, holding me tight as a contraction rushes through me. Being pregnant at sixteen isn't how I envisioned a life for myself but true love made me do it—along with raging hormones and non-existent self-control when I'm around Murphy—and a Catholic upbringing made me keep it. Her. We were told three months ago that we're going to have a little girl.

Even at sixteen, Murphy is all in. And if I hadn't understood it before the ultrasound, I definitely did when he cried at the news. Most guys dream of having boys for all the stereotypical reasons, but not Murphy. No, Murphy wanted a little girl because, according to him, she'd grow up to be strong and determined just like me and he couldn't imagine anything more incredible than that.

On the flip side, I am petrified. Everything about this situation scares me to the point of panic attacks. The first time I experienced what I thought was a contraction—turns out it was Braxton-Hicks—I actually thought I was having heart failure due to stress. Murphy talked me through it since he'd been reading all the books on having a baby and what to expect during the whole process. We'd curl up in bed, my head on his belly and his palm on mine—protective and soothing—as he read me chapters out loud that corresponded to my pregnancy month. It would always make me feel better.

Murphy always makes me feel better. The eye to my hurricane.

"Breathe, sweetie. In through your nose, out through your mouth." It's the second contraction of the day but they're too far apart for us to rush to the hospital. Besides, my dad's not here yet and he's the only one with a car.

"Can Murphy take us to the hospital, Mom? It really hurt!" It's gone now, only the remnants of pain are left, but just the anticipation of it coming back is making my mouth dry and my heart beat out of my chest.

When I look up at my mom, she's staring at the clock and I realize she's watching the minutes to see if another contraction is about to hit me. After five minutes of nothing, I come to the same conclusion as my mother... it's not time yet.

"Let's wait a little longer, okay? I spoke to Mary this morning and she mentioned Murphy had to work all day so he could take the next week off since that's your actual

due date." Her words hit me straight in the chest with both disappointment that he won't be here for another couple of hours and pride because his whole life already revolves around me and the baby.

It was never in my plans to get pregnant this soon but I guess my silver lining is Murphy, because there is no one else I would rather make such a beautiful mistake with than him.

"Okay, yeah. I'm better now, I think." I start to rise but gravity is getting the better of me in this position. My mother chuckles as she grabs on to the edge of the counter and lifts herself up before helping me rise to my feet. I've only got weight on my belly but damn, it's like my entire balance has been wonky for the last five months.

"Go lie down in our bedroom, the bed is firmer than yours, and I'll call you when dinner is ready." With a kiss to my forehead, she gently taps my belly, as she always does, before walking away.

When I first realized I was pregnant, my greatest fear was disappointing my parents. As an only child, all of their hopes and dreams were placed on me. Work hard, get good grades, go to college, get a good paycheck, then create a family.

That was the plan.

With my grades, I could follow Murphy to whatever college he was planning on attending—anywhere except the five boroughs since both of our parents had forbidden it. We knew it had something to do with the Irish and Italians not being able to stand in the same room without punches and insults being thrown at any given time. The words mafia and mob were never used in our presence but Murphy and I weren't stupid. Some of the guys hanging out with them looked like caricatures of those old Godfather movies.

We had set our sights on the University of Connecticut because it wasn't too far from our parents but far enough to keep our privacy. Plus, raising a family there seemed picture perfect and he and I deserve nothing less than that.

Obviously, the shock of the news was palpable. My father's face turned a bright red as he stared daggers at Murphy sitting next to me, his fingers wrapped around my trembling hand, and I remember thinking Daddy's cheeks matched his Red Sox jersey. My mother stayed silent for all of two minutes before she announced, "Well. God is clearly testing our love and faith and we Irish never back down from a challenge, now, do we?" And that was that.

My mom rose from her chair, came to my side, and placed a warm kiss on the top of my head as her hand tapped my still-flat belly twice.

It wouldn't be easy every day, but we would get through it because we had a support system. And I had Murphy.

I doubted his parents would react in the same way but, together, we could do anything.

As I walk up to my parents' room, I call out a quick, "Wake me up when Dad gets home, please," over my shoulder and smile when she sing-songs that she promises. My mom is quirky, not a negative bone in her body, and her faith in God and family is unshakeable.

And so was mine... until it wasn't.

I'm startled awake by a contraction but something, a bone-deep feeling I cannot explain, tells me to be quiet. It's in the air, the way the house feels as I open my eyes and focus on where I am and what is happening.

That's when I hear my mother's shrill voice screaming that she doesn't know.

"I don't know, I swear. I have no idea what you're looking for."

My goal is to sit up quickly but my belly won't allow it. Rolling to my side before sitting up on the edge of the bed, I quietly rise to my feet so I can check on my mom.

That's when I hear the boom of my father's voice. "What the fuck do you think you're doing in my house?" His words are immediately followed by the same crashing sound as when the plates fell to the floor with my contraction earlier. My mother screams again and a voice I don't recognize bellows throughout the house.

"Where's the fucking money?"

My eyes dart to the closet, knowing there's a hidden space behind my mother's clothes big enough for me to crawl into, even though the bag full of money is stashed in there.

My hands land on my stomach and, in that moment, I do what Murphy would want me to do. I protect our baby.

As quietly as I can, I crawl to the closet, gritting my teeth as another contraction spears through my nervous system, the weight of the baby in this position making things doubly uncomfortable. But I can't think about my pain right now. The only thing that matters is my baby's safety. The pounding feet on the stairs, accompanied by my mother's wails and my father's hurling insults make me pause only a half a second before I push through all of my fears and unlock the small door hidden by coats and dresses. If I hadn't found this place when I was younger, playing with my mother's shoes, I never would have guessed there was anything here. The tiny door is invisible; only by touching can you feel the imperfections.

Just as the bedroom door slams open, I hear the click of my safe space. Sitting back, I breathe through the pain of the *contraction, my back against the wall, my legs spread as far as I can get them, which isn't much.*

Outside, in the bedroom, the sounds of a struggle, the cries, and the threats, are clear as day. This cubby is safe but it's definitely not soundproof.

"Where's the fucking money? Before I not only kill your bitch but rape her first."

My mother spits insults at him, telling him that God will make him burn in the depths of Hell for his sins, but the cracking sound that follows tells me she's just been silenced by his hand—or his fist.

"Don't you fucking tou—" My father's voice stops abruptly as a deafening sound replaces it. I gasp into my hand because I know that sound. I've caused that exact sound before with my dad and Murphy—at a firing range.

Seconds pass with nothing but silence and that scares me more than anything, because if my dad's booming voice is gone then that means... oh God.

"Now, tell me where the money is and you can live to raise your whore of a daughter's baby. If you don't, I'll fuck your pretty little cunt then I'll find your little girl and fuck her pregnant cunt too while I make you watch." Fear makes my contractions triple in intensity but I don't dare make a

sound, biting my tongue enough to fill my mouth with my own blood.

"She's not here, you unholy Neanderthal. Do what you will but I can't tell you what I don't know." In that moment, I wonder if she's telling the truth because, if I know about the money, I can't imagine she doesn't. Is this money more valuable than her dignity? Her life?

My life?

Then it hits me.

She must have guessed I'm in here so giving the money's location would be giving mine and knowing my mother... yeah, my life is more important than hers.

Tears streak down my face as I continue to push through the pain now coming in continuous waves without giving me enough of a break to breathe through it.

"Suit yourself."

The banging on the wall confuses me until the hard rhythm reminds me of a boat on the sea, the waves hitting the wood at even intervals. Like the headboard of my parents' bed hitting the wall at a fast, even pace.

My hands are on my ears as I try my best to block out the sounds of my mother's dignity being ripped away from her. All I can hear is her praying.

"Our Father, who art in Heaven..." Over and over again she begs her God to keep her safe, to keep her soul safe, but I know, deep in the very fiber of my being, that she's praying to God to keep me and my baby safe.

When the intruder roars out his satisfaction and my mother's prayers grow louder and louder, everything stops and I freeze. My vagina is impossibly stretched and I've got the uncontrollable urge to push the baby out but I can't. I can't. I can't. If I do, she'll cry and we'll be found.

I have to protect us.

I have to save us.

I have to save her.

"Where. Is. The. Fucking. Money?"

My body is contorted in pain, my belly burning from my opening to my chest as I try to stop this birth until it's safe.

"I..." A deep, guttural sob escapes my mother's lips, the desperation hitting me deep in my soul. "Don't. Know."

"Suit yourself." He repeats his same ominous words before the sound of a gunshot echoes through the room. Knowing what's happening on the other side of the wall and not being able to do anything about it feels like I took a bullet, too. Something in me dies in that moment, leaving a void for a new me to be born, but my instinct to survive keeps me quiet.

I stay silent as the man rifles through my parents' bedroom, even inside the closet without ever touching the wall that hides me.

I stay quiet as he goes through the entire home, yelling out my name but getting no response.

I stay quiet as my body pushes out a baby that I've tried to protect all this time by not letting it out.

I stay quiet as the front door slams and silence follows.

I stay quiet as I finally, desperately, get myself and the baby out of the cubby hole and look for scissors to cut the umbilical cord.

But when my baby stays quiet throughout all of that, her eyes tightly closed, her mouth slightly open, I scream so loudly I'm surprised the walls didn't shake down through to the foundations.

Holding my baby to my chest, I walk out of the closet only to find a scene from a horror movie in front of me.

Blood. Blood is everywhere. On me, on the floor where my father's head is swimming in a pool of it. The bed, where my mother's spread legs are soaking from where her head wound has bled all over the covers.

A wall shuts down as I remember why she's dead. Why they're both dead.

Placing a kiss on my baby's forehead, I tell her I love her before I place her on the bed, a cover over her little body. Then I push my mother's bloody limbs together because I don't want her dignity to take another hit when whoever finds them sees her in this indecent position.

Then, with pain becoming a second skin and almost a companion, I grab the bag that my mother said she knew nothing about and walk to the door, not giving a second glance to my old life.

That memory slashes through my heart, my brain fighting to keep me sane as I try to drive this truck as fast as I can to save my daughter and Murphy.

One thing I can say is that Crank is a helluva mechanic because this beat-up truck took the abuse like a fucking champ. No amount of swerving, slamming of brakes, and break-neck speeding had any kind of effect on this monster. When I'm close enough to see Murph's place, I pull up against the curb, three houses down, and watch the house like a fucking hawk.

It's quiet, not a fucking soul around, which is normal for a little past two in the morning but still... nothing is sitting right with me and if there's one thing I trust, it's my gut.

The rumble of Flower's turbos draws my gaze to the rearview and I see her pulling up behind me. We both sit for a minute before slipping out of our vehicles and, with just a silent nod, cementing our earlier plan. I slink away into the night, using the shadows as my camouflage while Flower waits for Crank to arrive.

Because I'm not an idiot, I don't go in with guns blazing and ask questions later. That's ridiculous and only works in the movies. In real life, you assess your threat, recon, then regroup. Which is exactly what I do as I circle the house, hiding in the dark patches between the street lights. Wearing all black always helps. By the time I've assessed the whole place, I realize that, although it's late at night and in a family neighborhood where it's expected for everyone to be asleep, I'm surprised Murphy's light isn't on. The kind of adrenaline we just had injected from the fear of losing Hallie isn't something you get over that easily.

Then again, I'm no doctor and maybe he's just passed out from said adrenaline rush.

By the time I get back to our cars, Crank has arrived and he and Flower are organizing their strategy.

Time to fuck shit up... or not. Hopefully not. Hopefully the two most important people in my life are happy, sleeping and dreaming of better evenings than the one we had tonight.

Crouching against the side of Murphy's house, I nod to Crank and Flower, pointing to the back door with my chin while I do what anyone would expect if this is a trap—I knock at the front door.

Half expecting to get a rainfall of bullets fired at me, I step to the side just as my knuckles hit the green door twice. I'm almost disappointed when everything stays quiet. This need to kill, to make someone suffer for thinking they could take what's mine then send me on a wild goose chase, is enough to make me want to draw blood. Lots and lots of it.

When nothing happens, I reach into my pocket to text Crank a warning but realize my phone is with Glitch while he tries to triangulate the cell signal of whoever is trying to help me. Or ambush me... but that's a puzzle to solve later. The only thing I need to concentrate on at this point is making sure Murphy and Hallie are okay, then killing those responsible for this fucked up night.

Pulling out the pick from the inside pocket of my jacket, I push it into the lock, surprised it's already unlocked. If that's not a red flag, I don't know what is. Murphy would never leave the front door open. Not a fucking chance in

Hell would he leave the whole world with easy access to our daughter.

Where earlier I had doubts, I'm now fucking certain this is a trap, but it doesn't matter, I'm still going in. The loves of my life need me and I'll be damned if I disappoint them again.

Yes, *loves*. As in plural. It doesn't take a fucking genius to realize that my feelings for Hallie are tattooed inside my DNA and my love for Murphy never stopped, it was just on pause while the universe decided when to push us back together again.

I know, right? I didn't think I had a heart and it turns out it's still there; hidden beneath the cobwebs and dust but still functioning.

As quick as lightning, I kick the door in then jump to the other side, crouching and making myself as small as possible while, this time, the less imposing sound of multiple silencers redecorates the entrance of the house.

These motherfuckers are going to pay for the remodeling with their blood.

When I hear the back door slam open, I take advantage of the shouts of surprise and redirection of gun fire to slip inside.

Goddammit!

One of the fuckers wasn't stupid enough to run to the back and stayed, waiting for me to show myself. I grunt as a bullet slips by, grazing my jacket but missing me otherwise.

Pop!

The difference between me and this joker is that I don't miss.

Stepping over the body of an Irish piece of shit, I grab his gun and take cover behind the wall that leads to the kitchen, where the back door is wide open.

"Where the fuck is she?"

I'm right here, you fucking cunts.

Just as I'm about to aim at the two men in the kitchen, I feel the cold, hard metal at the back of my head that stops me in my tracks.

"She's right here, fellas. The bitch isn't so scary now, is she?" This motherfucker will be the last to die. Slowly. "Drop your fucking guns, you thieving little whore."

Oh yeah. Slowly and painfully.

The lights turn on just as I'm about to take my chances and drop kick him before putting a bullet in his balls.

I freeze. My jaw tightens with a hatred I've only ever reserved for one person.

Ronan fucking Callaghan in the flesh.

It's time to be smart because this motherfucker cares about fuck all, least of all me.

"Well, don't I feel all kinds of special." I drop the dead guy's silenced gun and my own Beretta, as well as the collection of knives around my thigh, before crossing my arms and staring back at Ronan, my sarcasm slapping him in the face.

"You ain't special in the least, little girl. Now, this is how it's going to go. I know it's been thirteen years so I'm guessing that money is long gone." He'd be right.

"I gave it to charity." I shrug like it's an obvious answer and enjoy—all too much—the deepening red tint of his pale skin matching the hue of what's left of his ginger hair. Can't say I'm surprised, this asshole wouldn't spare a look, let alone a dime, to someone in need.

"Hope it was worth it." Ronan looks over my shoulder to the dude holding me at gunpoint and narrows his eyes at him. "Where's Riley? Text him and tell him to get his ass over here." Oh, this is getting better by the second.

There's movement behind one of the two shooters in the kitchen, who are just watching us like we're the main attraction at an Ozzy Osbourne concert, and I don't need to see beyond my peripheral vision to know Crank and Flower have chosen this moment to surprise them.

Pop! Pop!

Two down.

"Checkmate." Crank's word brings a smile to my face as he holds a gun in each hand, both pointed at Ronan, while Flower slowly advances on douchebag here who, apparently, has a death wish.

"By the way, you fat fuck, I didn't come alone." Taking the stunned opportunity to get rid of this fucker behind me, I kick him in the kneecap just as Crank gets close enough to wrap a beefy arm around Ronan's throat while his other hand presses the barrel to his temple. As I slide to the side to place myself behind Ronan's guy, I pick up a gun and slide my favorite knife out of my right boot. Asshole should have patted me down for weapons. Guess he won't be making that mistake again.

True to my own word, I slice this guy's throat from one ear to the other and let him drown in his own blood, choking for air and grabbing at his wound like his fingers could possibly hold it in.

"Am I scary now, motherfucker?" I wink at his bulging eyes then turn my rage to Ronan, who's cool as a fucking cucumber.

"Where's Murphy? Where's Hallie? I promise, if you tell me now, I'll kill you nice and quick." I'm a bad liar but I do try.

Ronan whistles then smiles like a fucking lunatic.

That feeling in my stomach returns and I know for a fact that I'm not going to enjoy the next words out of his mouth.

"I was hoping not to have to use my plan B." It's like he doesn't have a two-hundred-pound madman almost cutting his air off, that's how calm and collected he is.

Coughing and spluttering at my feet, where the Irishman is bleeding out, distracts me for half a second and when I look up, I see them.

Murphy is the first to join us in the kitchen, a house of a man towering over his already-six-foot-three frame and pressing the barrel of his Colt at the back of my man's head. The grip on my gun tightens and I have to talk myself down from risking everything and shooting that big goon right between his beady eyes.

Instead, my guilty gaze falls to Murphy, whose features are tight, eyes alert and staring right back at me with a strength that I didn't know I needed him to project. From the shaking of my hands to the baring of my teeth, it's not difficult to see that I'm holding on to my temper and sanity by a thin thread. But Murphy gives a slight, almost imperceptible shake of his head to tell me to hold it together.

Immediately, I know why.

Behind him, a second goon shows up and this one has Hallie. With one meaty paw pulling her hair back so far she can barely see where she's walking, she struggles to follow his instructions.

"Come on, bitch, we ain't got all day." At his harsh words, my baby begins sobbing; her cheeks streaked with tears and saliva dripping from her mouth where the gag separates her lips. Again, Murphy tries to be the eye to my hurricane but I'm past that shit.

You do not make my baby girl cry. Fuck that.

"You, motherfucker," I point the blade of my knife to his acne-scarred face and wait until his attention is solely on me. "Will be the first to die." Then I point to the dying asshole at my feet, whose eyes are three seconds away from Hell, and spit. "You won't be as lucky as he is. I'll make sure *you* suffer."

All the men laugh and laugh but inside, I'm laughing the loudest because I always keep my fucking promises.

CHAPTER TWENTY-THREE

MURPHY

Fuck, even when she's covered in blood and shaking like an earthquake ready to destroy an entire city, she's the most mesmerizing woman I've ever seen. The only problem is that I need her to stay calm. For Hallie, for me. The only way to survive this shit show is for everyone to calm the fuck down and have a serious discussion about what the fuck is going on.

I can't see Hallie, she's behind me, but judging from the venom etched across J's features and the hitched sobs behind me, I'm guessing it's nothing good. With a guy holding a gun to my head, pushing me to scoot forward, it takes everything in me not to turn around and shove that gun down his throat. The only problem is that I don't want to mentally scar my daughter for the rest of her life by getting my brain shot out and splattered across the walls. So, for her, I bite the bullet... no pun intended.

Pulling out a stool from the kitchen bar, he pushes me down and when I lift my eyes, I can finally see Hallie. It's not hard to understand J's rage because it's suddenly coursing through my own veins, boiling hot and running fast. Our eyes meet and I try my best to soothe her, tell her with a forced smile that everything is going to be okay.

And it will be. It has to be.

We still have forever to live, all three of us. God wouldn't be so fucking cruel as to bring Jordyn into our lives just to take her away again. That's not an option.

Hallie's sobs slow, her chest heaving just a little less, but her tears still stream down her face like twin waterfalls. She's so young, so sheltered, that seeing her like this is like a kick to the gut. I've never been prone to violence and I've always kept my nose out of the mob's business but when this shit is over, I'm going to demand justice and it won't be with the fucking police or the courts.

"Let the boss go or one of them is going to die." At my captor's words, my eyes dart to J's, narrowing them so she reads my message loud and clear. If he goes free, we all die anyway.

J takes a menacing step toward us, her glare so glacial it could reverse global warming, and points her knife at the guy who's drilling a hole at the back of my head with his gun.

"Speak again and you'll be wearing this knife... in your right eye." Then she turns to Ronan, spreading her arms out wide like the angel of death, and pauses, waiting for everyone to have eyes on her. In any other scenario, she would be magical. Right here and now, she's deadly and never been more stunning. "What the fuck do you want? Seriously. You got me. I'm here. What the actual fuck do you need them for? After all these years of protecting them, now you decide to hurt them? It's me you want, Ronan. I'm right fucking here for the taking."

At her words, I lunge. It's instinct, like my body forgot to warn my brain that any threat to J is a threat to me. Except I don't make it an inch before I'm pulled back by the gag that's tied around my head and slammed back into the chair like I'm insignificant.

"It's not that simple, Jordyn. You took something from me that you can't give back. These two were my reimbursement, but I'm a businessman, I can negotiate the terms." J's man tightens his grip on Ronan, causing him to cough and narrow his eyes at her. "Be careful, little girl, wanting to play in a big boy world."

It dawns on me that Ronan has no idea who Jordyn works for. The revelation gives me hope because, knowing my girl, she's got a couple of safety plans already in place and these fuckers won't know what hit them.

J goes along with his game, bringing the edge of her knife up to her throat and scratching at the skin like she's soothing an itch. It makes me nervous, and when I look up at Hallie, I see her frown at her mother. I wish I could tell her not to worry, to trust Jordyn and her skills.

"All right, let's negotiate. You let them go and take me instead. I'll work for you until you think I've paid you back in jobs you need done." She shrugs like it's no big deal, but the tension at the corners of her eyes and the set of her shoulders tells me a completely different story. J's chomping at the bit and wishing she could sink her teeth into Ronan's carotid.

As much as I couldn't believe the Irish would do this to us, it was a wake-up call to see them come after us tonight. Ronan showed up with Hallie, the pale of her skin telling me everything I needed to know. When he busted into my house, he gave me the orders.

"When the phone rings, you tell her everything is fine. Do that and you both survive."

Yet here we are, everyone with a gun ready to kill or die.

"No deal. I've already got Riley for that." He does. Riley is loyal to his father, tonight was solid proof.

I watch as J's henchman leans into Ronan's ear and whispers something I can't hear, a smirk at the corner of his lips and a glint in his eyes.

"You fucking cunt whore!" Hallie and I both jump at the sudden howl coming from deep in Ronan's lungs, looking around trying to figure out what the fuck is going on. J scratches at the dip of her throat, running her knife down to her cleavage then back up again. The blood on her smears but it doesn't seem to faze her.

"He took what is mine."

Again with the shrugging, J just ignores the fact that we're both being held at gunpoint. At least, that's the act she's putting on.

"Sir, do we kill 'em?" my captor asks like it's a quiz and he doesn't want to fail.

"What's it gonna be, Ronan? Are you a real business-man or a fucking amateur?" J's pushing him and, for the first time, I'm afraid he'll take her offer and we'll lose her.

I can't let that happen.

Fighting against my restraints, I try to scream against my gag and let her know that we don't accept these terms. We can't lose her. Hallie would not be okay with this.

J ignores me and beefy fucknut here slams my face into the bar. The pain shoots from my nose all the way up to my brain and down my spine like a fucking lightning streak. Gritting my teeth as I lift my face, I'm met with red all over the place. Hallie screams, muffled behind the rag in her mouth, eyes wild and filled with terror.

J's head turns to me and I can tell by the way her gaze rises to the man behind me that she's about to go mental on everyone in here.

We need to stay calm, though. Ronan is not stable, his eyes are bulging with rage at whatever it is that J's guy said to him. All it would take is one word and we're gone.

"I'm a vengeful motherfucker, Jordyn O'Neill, and blood can only be repaid in blood." When Ronan utters his last sentence, I know we're all fucked. But why?

It all happens so fast that it's impossible to see it clearly.

Ronan turns to my captor and, with a face hard and unforgiving, gives the order. "Kill them." But before anything else happens, the kitchen door flies open and the lights go out, leaving us all in the dark.

The whizzing of bullets and muzzle flash from the guns are all around me, my mind focused on one thing only... Hallie. I need to get to her, make sure she's not caught in the crossfire. Keep her safe. That's my only job, the only one that counts.

Ducking my head, I swivel the stool and grab for the gun that was just pointed at my head. The guy's got both pounds and inches on me so the struggle is fucking real, but I've got adrenaline on my side boosted by my never-ending need to keep my baby girl safe. I'd say we're evenly matched.

Just as I get a punch in, my fist connecting with something that feels a lot like a jaw, I simultaneously hear the sound of a gun going off then feel the searing pain in my chest. The shot seems far away and the pain feels like an arrow sloshing through muscle.

I'm fine though and as soon as I'm free from his grip, I crawl to Hallie. Or at least to where she was before the lights went out. There's shuffling, running, grunting, and something that sounds a lot like a knife going in and out of flesh. I don't give a fuck, though. The only thing I care about is Hallie.

"Hallie, where are you, baby?" This is what I try to say, but only garbled noises actually come out of my mouth because I can't get the fucking rag out. The noise is insane and I'm guessing it won't take long before the police are here with an ambulance and the fire department because, with all these shots going off, something is bound to catch fire.

"Daddy!" Her voice is like a choir of angels singing in my ear and lighting a path for me to go to her. I follow it, on my knees and with my arms still tied behind my back. The pain in my chest is growing and my breath is slowing. I'm slipping left and right in my panic to get to Hallie, no doubt blood from my nose bleed and probably from the others too.

"Daddy, please!" I hear her just as I reach out for her and, together, we take advantage of the chaos to hide out in the makeshift closet under the stairs.

Hallie reaches for me, feeling her way to my mouth to take off the gag, then hugs me tight to her and cries in the crook of my neck. I want to hold her but I can't.

"Sweety." Why does my voice sound so croaked? "Can you untie my hands?"

Hallie doesn't answer, just nods in my neck and twists her small frame around me to loosen the ropes and finally free me. As soon as I feel them fall, I take her in my arms and squeeze her like she's my lifeline.

"Daddy, why are you all wet?" Am I? Oh, right. The nosebleed.

"I think he broke my nose." Hallie holds me tighter still and we both find comfort in this little refuge while all fucking Hell breaks loose.

There are voices screaming out orders beyond the door. Some are J's, others are Ronan. Two more shots ring out then nothing.

I freeze, not having a clue as to who is going to be opening that door and greeting us on the other side.

"Shh, baby. Don't make a noise."

Hallie holds her breath, her little body shaking like a fucking leaf, and it enrages me that those fuckers put her through this. I try to hold my breath but it's getting too hard to move my chest, to breathe even. In fact, the pain is everywhere and I have a feeling it's not just my nose.

Outside, the lights go on and, with it, relief fills every inch of my body when I hear J calling out for us. She sounds feral, desperate to see us.

I bang on the door and, not a second later, it's ripped open and the most heartbreaking and beautiful face I've ever seen fills my entire vision.

"It's safe, you can both come out but, Hallie, you need to close your eyes, okay?" J's voice is like a balm to my soul. Aloe vera to my burns.

As my adrenaline starts coming down, I realize my head is unnaturally heavy but I have to get Hallie out of here, take her away from what I'm guessing is carnage outside this room.

"Come on, baby girl. Let your mother take you. I'll be right behind you." Hallie is clinging to me, her arms squeezing my neck and sobbing on my shoulder. "We can't get out together but I promise to have you back in my arms as soon as we're out, okay?" That gets her attention, prompting her to unwrap herself from me and scoot over to her mother. As soon as she's crossed the threshold, I try to pull myself up but my body won't cooperate. Every move I make is a spear to my chest, adding to the ongoing throb of my nose.

"What the fuck? Murphy!"

My brows furrow at the panic in J's voice.

Jordyn never panics. She's the definition of level headed, or at least that's her brand of resting bitch face. Why is she yelling at me?

"Come here, Murph. Can you get yourself out?"

I blink at her, wondering what the hell she's talking about. Of course I can get out. I made this space with my bare hands, built it and furnished it. I can crawl out of it.

My leg is bent and I try to straighten it out so I can crawl out of this small space but it just falls over, taking me with it.

Fuck. Why did I just fall over?

"Crank! Get the fuck over here. NOW!" J's screaming, the panic has risen to something else and... is that Hallie screaming, too? What the fuck is going on?

Everything is slippery beneath me and I see nothing but blurriness above me.

"Murph, look at me. Look at me, please."

I try to force my gaze to follow J's voice, but everything feels so heavy. Then J's face is above me, looking down like an angel. Her steel-blue eyes tell me a million things and yet not the words I want to hear. Her smile is fake and the worry she's trying to hide is visible at the corners of her eyes.

"You stay with me, Murph. Do you hear me? You do not get to bow out. Not now. Not ever."

I don't know why I say what I say next, but it feels like the right time, somehow.

"I love you, J. Every day since the first time I pulled your pigtails and said you looked like a princess." Something wet falls on my cheek and when I focus on J's face, I see the tears. More than anything else tonight, that single drop of salty water scares the shit out of me.

"Then you asked me if you could be my prince." Yeah, I did that. The fact she remembers is enough for me. She loves me, she always has because a love like ours doesn't die, it only grows bigger until it becomes life itself.

"Oh my God, Daddy!"

"Pull him out and carry him to the truck. Flower, call Stefano and get me the closest address for a doc."

I love J's voice, even when she's giving orders. It's firm, yet sexy and inviting, with a hoarse quality to it like she's trying to seduce you and kill you at the same time.

I think I'm being carried. All I see is movement but nothing is clear, like watching the countryside while riding on a speeding train. I know it's my ceiling but it's just a flash of nothing.

"Put him in the back. Hallie, you stay with him, all right? Make sure he doesn't fall asleep." Who can't fall asleep? Me?

"Daddy, please, don't close your eyes." It suddenly dawns on me that I'm lying on my back, my head resting on Hallie's thighs as our bodies take off like a bullet. Hallie's face is all I see and, for that, I'm grateful. She's my greatest achievement.

"Hey, baby girl."

"Dad, you can't talk. You have to keep your strength, okay?" I nod because she's scared and I don't want her to be. She needs reassurance and that's my job, I intend to do it well.

Raising one of my hands to my chest, I feel the wetness, my pain almost debilitating as my fingers find a hole in my shirt that goes straight through my flesh. Fuck, this can't be good.

"Is he awake, Hallie?" J. Jordyn. She's worried. So am I, to be honest.

"Yes, but his eyes are fluttering open and closed."

"Hallie." My voice is barely audible against the noise of this vehicle. Jesus, how old is this thing?

"Shhh, Daddy. Keep your strength."

Despite the blood on my fingers, I reach up for Hallie and bring her face closer to mine.

"Listen to me, okay?"

She nods, tears running down her face like a stream in a rainstorm.

"You are everything. The stars and the moon and the entire universe can't hold a candle to the goodness in your soul." I cough and a copper taste invades my mouth but I have shit to say and I need to get this out, just in case. "I am so incredibly proud of you. Proud to be your father."

"Mom! Please hurry! Oh my God, Dad, stop talking!" I shake my head but the numbness makes it impossible to control my actions, so I gather all my strength and focus only on her.

"We're almost there, just hang on. You fucking hang on, Murphy."

I smile at J's words, her emotions a true testament to her feelings for me. For us.

We're not done yet. After everything we've been through, we deserve to be a family.

"Daddy, please, just hang on for me, okay? Don't leave me, please, please, please, don't leave me. I don't think I can live without you." I shake my head because, if I don't make it, she needs to keep going. She needs to live... for me.

"You can and you will. You need to take care of your mother because she..." I cough again and, this time, I almost choke on my own blood. I know it's blood in my throat because it's like drinking water from old pipes. "She's going to need you."

Hallie shakes her head, sobbing and begging me to stay with her as my eyes grow heavy and tired.

"We're here! You fucking hang on because we're here!" I smile at J's words, happy to know that everything is going to be okay.

My girls and I will be together and our forever will be epic.

CHAPTER
TWENTY-FOUR

J

"**C**ome on, Kid, we need to get your dad inside." Hallie's clinging to Murphy like he's her lifeline, as if loosening her grip on him is crippling to her, and it breaks my fucking heart to watch her shaking her head.

It's taking everything I have to not scream, to not shout, to not track down the snake that is Ronan fucking Callaghan and skin the bastard for what he's done.

"He-he's not moving. Why isn't he moving? Dad? Daddy? Wake up, Daddy." Hallie's broken words are like a dagger to my soul, but she's young. This amount of blood is scary at the best of times, but he'll be okay. We just need to get him inside.

"Crank, move her. We need to get Murphy inside. Now!" My chest is heaving, adrenaline coursing through my veins, urgency pushing at every instinct I have.

"Boss..."

"I said, move her, Crank. We can't stand around. Get him in the fucking house."

Hallie's cries aren't slowing down and I don't blame her. In fact, I envy her ability to display every emotion so freely.

"No! Put me down!" She's struggling to break free of Crank's grip as Tab steps up to the truck, moving in to grab Murphy. "Daddy!"

"Boss..." Tab's usually steady voice is shaky, unsure as he stands to his full height with slumped shoulders.

"What?" I'm frustrated that he's not moving, not hurrying to get Murphy into the house for the doc.

It's a secluded location so Hallie's cries are luckily not drawing any more unwanted attention.

My eyes are on Tab, blocking out the cries from my daughter to pay attention to what is obviously so much more important than the job at hand. Then my stomach sinks as he shakes his head, lowering his eyes in an apology that I don't want.

I won't believe it. I can't believe it.

My heart is thumping at an impossible rate, my head pounding, my body shaking, my vision blurring as I shove Tab aside. "Move." I climb into the back of the truck to do what needs doing myself. "Come on, Murph." He's pale, his eyes closed from the blood loss, no doubt, as I grab him under the arms and heave him out of the car. "Don't just stand there, Tab. Help me."

Murphy's legs slide out of the car after him and Tab immediately lifts them, following me silently into the open door of the house where the doc is waiting.

"First door on the left."

I follow the doc's instructions, adrenaline being the only thing giving me strength right now, and head into the side room with a bed in the center. There are medical-looking tables and equipment beside it, and the doc follows us in as we gently place Murphy on the bed.

Hallie's cries are quieter now, subdued somewhat, and I'm thankful. She doesn't need this kind of pain in her life.

"Looks like a head injury and a shot to the chest. Bullet's still in there, no through hole." I'm to the point with my description of his wounds, needing the doc to get to work quickly. The fact that Murph has passed out isn't a great sign.

Pacing the rough-carpeted floor, I take a deep breath and wait for the doc's assessment as he does whatever medical doctor checks he needs to do. Feeling for a pulse and... wait, why isn't he...

"J, he's gone. We're too late."

No.

I did not hear that right.

"Check a-fucking-gain." I move over to the bed, grabbing Murph's wrist and feeling for a pulse myself... I check his neck... my mind is racing and my own heart is banging so hard against my chest that I can't feel Murph's heartbeat under my fingertips. Placing my head on his chest, I listen closer, putting my palm under his nose to check his breathing.

He's not moving.

His heart isn't beating.

There are no breaths.

I can't...

I just can't...

This isn't happening. Not again.

"Doc, do something!" My voice is a scream to even my own ears. "Fucking do something! Stop fucking staring at me and save him!" I press the heel of my hand to the center of Murphy's chest, placing my other palm over it, and begin chest compressions. Pushing down on his chest before giving two rescue breaths and trying again.

I don't know how long I do this for, all I do know is that tears are streaming down my face with every compression that doesn't bring him back.

"Come on, Murph. We have a daughter and she needs her dad to see her grow up." Two more breaths. Back to compressions. "Someone to see her off to prom." Breaths. Compressions. "Someone to walk her down the aisle on her wedding day." Breaths. Compressions. "Someone to call Grandpa when she has kids of her own." Breaths. Compressions. "And I need you too, Murph. Come on." Breaths. Compressions. "Please, Murph. Please. Come on."

"J... J..."

I don't know who it is, but someone touches my arm and I look down to see Murphy's hands... limp on the bed, a meaty palm on my elbow.

"Get the fuck off me." Breaths. Compressions.

The meaty hand disappears and the room is silent except for my heavy breaths, my panting, my exhaustion, my entire body breaking down because I failed. My roar is a guttural cry to the heavens, my head is spinning, my hands are shaking. I can't...

I sag across Murphy, covering his body with my own, his blood mingling with the blood already smeared across me.

There's a little girl in the other room who just lost her dad and it's my fault. No, actually, it's Ronan Callaghan's fault. The fucking Irish mob. Because they're greedy cunts who fucked over my parents then got mad at their revenge. This whole stupid mess is revenge upon revenge and it's fucking ridiculous. Closing my eyes, I let my mind flash images of Murphy—smiling, laughing, caring for our daughter—and vow deep down in my soul that this fucked up cycle will end with me.

Knowing what to do with a kid doesn't come naturally to me, but I need to do what Murph would want, what he would expect. I'm gonna fuck the kid up, but I'm all she's got now.

Shit this is too fucking painful.

Slowly, I peel myself away from Murphy's still body and put every bit of training I've ever had into use. I take a deep breath, grab a rag from the table to wipe at my face, blood smears and tears all over it.

The doc isn't in the room with us anymore, neither is Tab. I don't know when they left or how long I've been in here gripping at the man I thought I'd have a future with, a family.

I need to speak to my daughter.

Fuck, this has got to be the worst thing I've ever done.

With another deep breath, I press a light kiss against Murphy's forehead, stroking the short hair off his face, and walk away.

Hallie is in the main living space, in the arms of someone I never expected to see here. River is holding my little girl so tightly, rocking her back and forth like a baby, comforting her as the small sobs continue to fall from her lips. Marco is standing in the corner talking with the doc, Tab, Crank, Flower, and Binx are hovering close by, too afraid of our don to approach him.

River looks up as I step into the room, everyone else completely ignoring me as if they know that what I'm about to do requires all my strength. I have no reserves for bullshit with anyone else.

It's all for her now.

Tipping my head to River, I approach, and she smiles the saddest kind of smile known to man, empathy clear in her bright green eyes. I sit next to her on the couch and she slowly moves Hallie over to me, her tiny arms wrapping around my neck as she clings to me.

"Did you..." Hallie sniffs and hiccups. "Did you save him, Mom?" Oh, God, I thought my heart had already broken in that room with Murphy.

This is worse.

River stands and I see her gesturing to the others before they all leave the room. Alone again.

Hallie's big hazel eyes, the perfect mix of her father and me, are focused on my face, which I know must be scary for a thirteen-year-old girl considering the blood coating me. Some of it being her father's.

She wants answers. The good news I fucking prayed for. Me... praying.

"No, baby girl. We've... lost him." My voice hitches as I speak, watching her tiny face crumble into a million pieces and the cry that leaves her throat will stay with me forever. She shakes uncontrollably, gripping on to me so tightly, letting out every pain she's feeling with cries and screams and tears.

I cry right along with her, breaking down my walls for this precious little girl in my arms, letting her witness the side of me I'd kill anyone else for seeing.

And we break together.

It's right here and now that I vow to end this once and for all. Ronan Callaghan will die. By my hand. As will every other member of the Irish mob in New Jersey.

And this little girl whose heart is breaking, shattered, forever changed, will never have to experience this kind of pain again.

CHAPTER
TWENTY-FIVE

J

My entire life I've only had to take care of myself and follow the Mancini orders—to be executed as I please. I've come and gone as I pleased, fucked who I chose, and lived where I felt best at home.

It's been barely twelve hours since we lost Murphy and my entire existence is now focused on this little girl—teenage girl—wrapped around me like a baby monkey, refusing to let me go. I should be out there chasing down Ronan, thinking of a million ways to peel the skin off his bones and feed it to him, but anytime I think about moving, Hallie just hangs on tighter.

No matter what is happening outside this room, I can't deny her. It's impossible to even think about it.

A soft knock at the door has me shifting on the bed, Hallie's arms and legs pinning me down so that all I can do is crane my neck to see who it is.

Stefano—the do-it-all man for the Mancini family for as long as I can remember—slowly opens the door, his kind face peeking in and mouthing for permission to come in. I don't bother whispering, Hallie's awake, has been for a while. As far as everyone living in this Upper East Side, old money mansion is concerned, we're not to be disturbed unless it's life threatening or life sustaining. Marco and River's home has become our haven and I don't think I could ever thank them enough for their generosity.

"Come on in, Stefano." My voice is unrecognizable, like I've been drinking and singing at the top of my lungs all night long. I haven't, of course, but stranger than that, I've been crying right along with Hallie. I'm not sure if my tears are from losing Murphy or because my baby girl's suffering is so bone deep. Her wails are such pure and unadulterated agony, that I can feel them straight to my core. Either way, I know exactly what she's feeling. The only difference is that when my parents were killed, I ran. I ran to save myself. I ran from the vision. I ran from the devastation of losing my baby.

I ran, but Hallie is staying and dealing with her loss. The least I can do is be there, for once.

"I've brought you both some breakfast. Signorina Hallie needs to eat or hunger will feed her pain." I know he means well but I don't think her lack of food is feeding her pain. I'm pretty sure her lack of a father is the cause, but I just nod and thank him for being so thoughtful.

Placing one hand on Hallie's forearm, he pats her like a grandfather would, then looks down at me and smiles a sad, sad version of his usually bright grin. His empathy knows no bounds, and in my vulnerable state, I feel the pricking of tears welling up all over again as he nods his understanding to me.

As he walks away, I realize something important, something I've probably known this whole time but was too focused elsewhere to notice; I have a family.

River and Marco, Stefano, Lina and her crazy trio of possessive men, my Reapers.

Hallie.

They are all my family and I have to make sure they know that I'll be okay. It's been a while since I've done anything but wander alone, but I'm pretty sure family worries about family, and Stefano making sure my daughter is well fed is his way of showing me how much he cares.

"Hallie, sweetheart, we need to eat." I don't move except for a hand stroking her head, over and over again.

"Idon'twantto." Her answer is a mumble into my neck and I only understand because it's the same answer she's given me for every question I've asked.

"We have to stay strong for him, baby girl. I have things I need to get done and I'm hoping you'll help me, if you can." I figured including her in Murphy's funeral preparations will help her to say goodbye to him, but what the fuck do I know?

For the first time in hours, Hallie's limbs untangle from me and her head rises from the crook of my neck. The sight of her makes my heart sink all over again. Red-rimmed eyes that make her hazel irises seem dull and muddy, her usually flawless skin is blotchy from her cheeks to her chin, but worst of it all is her perfectly pert nose, raw from rubbing at it like she's had the flu.

Despite all this, when she meets my gaze, there's a spark there I hadn't noticed at first. A hardness I've never seen before, ever. Something has changed and it's the opposite of healing.

"Can I help you kill the man who murdered my dad?" The breath in my lungs whooshes out, her words having the same effect as a punch to the gut.

"What?" I can barely whisper that one word because her request feels blasphemous coming from her innocent lips. God, no. I can't be the reason she turns out like me.

"I want to kill him. Ronan. I don't know if he's the one who actually shot Dad but I want to kill him." Her words end on that broken last syllable and all pretenses of being capable of ending a life die on a sob.

My poor baby... how am I supposed to help her heal if my own veins are screaming for retribution?

"I won't betray him, Hallie, and letting your hands get dirty would be the greatest treason to his memory." At my words, Hallie's arms and legs go back to monkey mode, making herself comfortable in a position I'm sure she associates with safety. It's then I remember Murphy's ritual and even though I still don't understand it, I reproduce it... for him, for his memory.

My lips on the top of her head, I whisper, "Sweet dreams full of fictional book boyfriends, baby girl."

Then I suffer like only a parent does as she cries herself to sleep for the next couple of hours.

I, however, stay awake the whole time, planning the greatest hit of my life. I only wish I could kill Riley all over again for stabbing his so-called best friend in the back.

For two days, we don't leave the room, or the bed for that matter, except to pee. We pick at Stefano's food, eating in silence as we both stare out the window into the gray Manhattan winter sky.

It's snowing again, which seems fitting. Snow always quiets The City down like a white blanket sucking away all the sounds. I appreciate it, thankful that Murphy would have this moment of peace with his soul.

"He was Catholic." I turn at the sound of Hallie's broken voice but don't interrupt her. "We never went to church, though. He said his faith was all around him and he didn't need to bow to any man to show his love to God." I nod because it sounds so like Murphy. Unlike him, I don't believe in anything but myself and, well, my love for Hallie.

"Do you know where he'd like to be buried?" I figure there's a plot somewhere with his grandparents, maybe.

Fuck. I can't believe I haven't thought of this sooner but...

"We need to call my grandparents." Hallie turns to look at me, the mention of Murphy's parents opening up the dam and making her crumble all over again.

"Yeah, baby girl, we do. I'll take care of it, okay?" My hand, the one not greasy with bacon delight, rubs soothing circles on her back as she leans into me and rests her weary head on my shoulder.

"I should do it and we need to lie to them." My spine turns to steel at her words, not sure why this is necessary. In fact, they should know that the Irish mob is responsible for the horror of losing their child.

"Lie about what, exactly?" I use my calm voice, the one that shows zero emotion, in fear of spooking her.

"You. I don't think they ever forgave you for abandoning me. And if we tell them what happened, they'll blame you." Hallie raises her head and looks straight into my eyes. What I see isn't a thirteen-year-old girl whose only worries are hanging out with her friends and doing well in school. There's something new, something darker, swimming in the depths of her eyes and I hate that it's there.

She's come face to face with the grim reality of life and it's taken a piece of her innocence and smashed it into tiny shards.

"But, Hallie…" I try to find an argument to her logic but it's not that easy.

"If they blame you, they'll fight to take me away from you and I can't lose another parent."

Goddammit. She's right, but also… would it be so bad? I mean, she'd be safe in Florida with her grandparents, far away from the Irish mob. She'd be down there enjoying life while I purge Newark of their filthy presence.

But then what?

Would Murphy's parents ever give her back to me? Would they use legal avenues to take her away permanently? Because as far as the government is concerned, I don't exactly exist anymore. Not on paper, at least.

Looking around the room we've holed ourselves up in for the last forty-eight hours, I make the decision I should have made thirteen years ago. I stay. I fight for my daughter with her by my side.

I'm older now, wiser, definitely stronger mentally and physically. Not only can I protect my daughter, I will do so with every last breath in my lungs.

"Okay, Hals, we'll tell them it was a car accident. Drunk driver, both killed in the accident." I make a mental note to have Glitch conjure up a coroner's report that declares Murphy's death as a traffic accident.

"Yeah, it'll save them the heartache of having to blame someone and then fight them in court or something." I nod but she can't see me, her head still resting on my shoulder, my hand still rubbing circles on her back.

"We'll be okay, Hals. We'll learn to be okay." To be honest, I'm not sure who I'm trying to reassure. Her or me.

"We'll never be okay because Dad was the best human in the world and now the world has to live without him." I don't argue, there's nothing to argue about. She's one hundred percent correct and this world, like my soul, will be a little less bright without his presence than it was two days ago.

"Let's take a shower, maybe start with that. I'll get Flower to bring all your things here from home. This is the safest place we can be, I promise you."

I know there are steps to this grief thing, but what I don't understand is why some of the steps keep coming back. I wish I could have the feeling, deal with it, then go to the next.

Like anger. That motherfucker is pissing me off. It comes and goes and just when I think I'm breathing through the loss of him, anger comes right back around and stabs me in the fucking heart. In the exact place Murph took a bullet.

Glitch tapped into some chatter about Ronan finding Riley exactly where we intentionally left him and burying him in the family cemetery. We needed this information so we could have the funeral on the same day to avoid any retaliation. Personally, I wanted to head down to that church and blow the whole fucking thing up into the sky and watch them all burn on their way down to Hell.

Marco vetoed that idea, his rational side clearing my own fog and helping me to see that having them busy on the other side of Newark was the only way to give Murphy's parents a proper funeral, no suspicions raised.

I hate him for being right.

Jonathan and Mary Gallagher haven't spoken a fucking word to me since they arrived yesterday following Hallie's phone call. They haven't insulted me, screamed at me, blamed me for anything. No, they have literally turned their backs on me every time to speak with Hallie, like I'm not even there.

Fortunately, my emotions are on lockdown throughout the entire funeral, my senses on high alert just in case Marco was wrong and some Irish fuckers decide to pay us a visit while armed to the teeth.

I could insert myself in the conversations but I don't have the mental space for it, and pretending to give a fuck has never been a skill I've acquired. Instead, I hold Hallie's hand and squeeze it every time her sobs burst out from the kind words of the priest.

My mind is hyper focused on every movement in my peripheral vision—every dancing leaf, every moving car, every person shifting in their seats.

"Why are there so few people here? Murphy was loved by the community." Mary's question is aimed at her husband but it's loud enough to be an accusation thrown at me. I want to answer her, tell her the very fucking people who supposedly loved him are the ones that killed him, but I keep my promise to Hallie and grit my teeth instead.

"I forgot to make an announcement, Grandma, I'm sorry." Hallie takes the blame and that shit just makes me angrier and angrier.

But then the cherry wood coffin is lowered into the ground, thoughts of everything just evaporate from my mind and all I see is the only man I've ever loved disappearing from sight forever.

The sorrow that envelops my entire torso is almost debilitating but I have to be here for Hallie, because whatever pain I'm feeling, hers is exponentially greater.

So, I do my job. The only job that really matters.

In that split moment in time, I become a mom. Not just a biological transformation from giving birth, but a transcendental change in the very fiber of my soul as my greatest focus becomes Hallie Gallagher. Until my dying breath.

We sit in the unforgiving cold for over thirty minutes after everyone has left, just staring at the bump in the ground that has covered up Murphy's soulless body, each of us holding a long-stemmed white rose. Everyone there dropped theirs in his grave but we just sit here, staring.

"He has a computer with everything in it. All his work, all the names and dates and whatever else on spreadsheets." Hallie's words shock me out of my own head, memories of Murph and I growing up together, falling in love, making love for the first time. Him kissing my belly when I told him I was pregnant, telling me it was a gift from God, and me scoffing, saying something about God not having to raise it and go to school at the same time.

"How do you know this?" My question is low, our conversation only for us.

"He told me all about it a few days before it all went down. I think he had a feeling." She looks at me, her pretty hazel eyes swimming in her never-ending streams of tears.

"I promise you, Hallie, if it's the last thing I do..." Placing my palms on either one of her wet cheeks, I make sure she sees the truth and the promise in my eyes. "I will take them all down. One kill at a time for the one kill they never should have taken."

Hallie nods, satisfied with my promise, and as if we've both had the same thought, we turn to Murphy and rise to our feet. As I hold out the rose in my hand to drop on top of freshly turned dirt, I flinch at the tiny stab in my finger.

"You okay?" Hallie looks at my hand as I throw the rose down and bring my finger to my mouth, sucking away the drop of blood.

"Yeah, just pricked my finger."

Hallie smiles at me then looks to the ground, a grin lifting the corners of her mouth, changing her features back to the little girl I met just a month ago.

"Any time I pricked my finger, Dad used to say it was the rose wanting to become my best friend. It was stupid but it made me feel better." I smile at her, hoping to see her happy again one day. But then she breaks down once more and I know it'll be a long time before we're okay.

As we walk away, arm in arm, I feel a vibration in my back pocket. Everyone I know was at the funeral but they left before me. My hope is that Glitch found something, anything, to feed my hunger for blood.

Taking out my phone as I open the truck door, I frown at the screen.

Unknown: I'm sorry for your loss.

Fucking hell, I need to know who this fucker is and I need to know now. Except I don't have time to waste on this anonymous Robin to my shadowy Batman because Hallie's voice has every hair on my back standing on end.

"Mom?" My glare shifts from the screen on my phone to her line of sight, my body instantly on high alert as I watch four brutish assholes approach us.

"Stay behind me." As I growl out my words, I'm already pushing her behind me, my free hand on the knife secured at my hip.

"What do they want?"

I don't answer Hallie since I have no idea who these fuckers are but I know an ambush when I see one. They're walking in a half moon, their stares on me like I'm a flight risk and their only job is to take me in.

Well, I hope they've brought reinforcements because I won't be taken down so easily.

"Mom, there's two more behind us." Hallie's trembling voice is no longer filled with grief but with unmasked fear.

Fuck, I guess they did the math and figured six against one seemed fair.

"You boys come for the funeral? I'm sorry to say, it's over now." I angle our bodies so that I can see all six men at once, a huge oak tree at our backs. "But feel free to pay your respects." One of them sneers, the corner of his mouth ticking up and showing a missing incisor. All of them have shaved heads and half have already broken their noses once or ten times.

"Give us the girl." So convinced they were here to kill me, it takes me a second to realize they're after Hallie. Yeah, I don't fucking think so.

"Hey, Hallie? You feel like going with these assholes?" Hallie just burrows deeper behind me, making herself as small as possible between me and the tree trunk. "Sorry, guys. No can do." I'm kicking myself for not bringing my gun to the funeral; figured I didn't need to have that on me for this but, clearly, I was wrong.

"Wasn't a question, bitch." Missing tooth guy must be the ringleader of this low-IQ circus since he's the only one capable of stringing two words together.

"Ah, see... I have a rule about leaving my daughter with misogynist pricks, so that's hard no from me." As discreetly as I can, I hand my phone back to Hallie, whispering, "Marco," and hoping she understands.

I need back up.

"Suit yourself."

At his words, I turn to Hallie, our eyes meeting in a brief window of time before all fucking Hell breaks loose.

"Run."

"No." Shaking her head, tears running down her face and lips trembling as she tries so fucking hard to be strong, I curse as the searing pain in my thigh hits me at the same time as the pop from the gun.

"Run!" I scream the one word out again but it's too late.

The six guys approach us like they're circling a wounded, feral animal, all of them aiming guns at us. I can't understand why they'd want her.

"Who sent you?" It's just as the words leave my mouth that movement on the cemetery's path steals my attention.

A black sedan with tinted windows slowly rolls up and stops just feet away from us as two of the guys grab me at the same time as two others tear Hallie away from me.

I stab them both in quick succession, aiming at their livers, hell, any vital organ will do at this point. I know my leg is bleeding but I'm pure adrenaline, fighting for my daughter's life. Plus, I've been hurt worse than this and still come out victorious.

"Fucking cunt, she stabbed me!"

No shit, asshole.

It's only when the knife is slapped out of my hand and a meaty arm is wrapped around my throat that I start kicking and snapping my head back to break their noses again.

"Mom!" Hallie's howl wounds me worse than the fucking bullet, prompting me to fight even harder.

In my struggle, I hope they're taking me with her. I can handle that, as long as we're together. Except it's immediately clear, as I watch two men dragging a kicking and screaming Hallie off to the car, that I'm of no interest to them whatsoever. Instead, the rest of these fuckheads are holding me down and laughing as I try desperately to get to my daughter.

"Hallie!" I scream back, my heart being ripped right out of my chest all over again as I see her arms reaching out for me, begging me to save her, pleading with her eyes to get her away from those two men.

One of the windows begins to roll down and there, framed by the shiny black of the sedan, is the cold, unmoving face of Murphy's mother.

"You ain't so scary after all, huh?" I'm frozen still, watching them almost throw Hallie into the car, her screams loud enough to reach my buzzing ears. "Grandma and Grandpa will take good care of her, it's where she belongs. Now, we were hopin' to get to kill ya but they said it would cause an all-out war with the Italians and we don't want that."

Once the car is out of sight, I turn my glare to the henchmen and grin like a psychopath who's just smelled fresh blood.

"No, you don't. Yet, here we are."

At my words, they all scoff. One Tooth Guy pushes me to the ground and slams his foot to my ribs, laughing like he's playing soccer with his pals. Another places his heel to my thigh, pressing on the bullet wound and helping the blood to spill quicker than I'd like. The others follow suit as I grunt and hiss with every blow to my body.

All the while, I stare at them, not giving them an ounce of my pain. Instead, I memorize their faces, every little detail of their ugly fucking mugs.

Pop! Pop!

Two of them drop to the ground as I turn to my back and stare up at the sky between the rustling branches of the oak tree, mentally thanking Hallie for sending out the message to Marco. He called for my Reapers and just like a tight-knit family, we always come for our brothers and sisters. Our boss can't show his face in Newark, it's not his territory, but I'm willing to bet that this little Irish stunt is going to wake up some sleeping monsters from the other side of the Hudson.

As I move, trying to stand, I watch as the skinhead goons run for their lives while heavy footsteps come running toward me. My phone bumps into my hand and, without thinking twice, I pick it up, the screen lighting up with a message from my crew saying they're on their way.

Then I remember the message from my anonymous Robin and grit my teeth.

Which loss is he talking about? Was he talking about Murphy or did he know this was about to happen?

In any case, it's all too little, too late.

Me: Fuck you.

To be continued in One Love – Book 2 of The Reapers Mafia Crew duet https://geni.us/TheReapers2

THE BLONDE ONE

I'm about to get sentimental, so bear with... Brunette and I began plotting this duet while we were writing The Escort series. It was supposed to be our second series, but Lina and her men demanded our attention first. We started writing this book after a teeny break, and a lot was going on in my personal world. A few chapters into the book, tragedy hit and I lost my mum to cancer after a three-month battle in hospital. I watched her last breaths while we listened to Motown after only days before telling her all about our plans for J's duet. My mum read every one of our books, and owned a personalised signed copy of each. She was one of our biggest fans and it's super sad that she won't get to read the final draft.

While this is going on, another member of our book community is battling the big C herself. Kat Elley is a warrior, going through chemo and still soldiering on, a smile always on her beautiful face.

These are just two reasons for our dedication for this book, plus the many others going through similar situations. We want you to know, we will always be on the other end of an email or message for each of you.

I mean, we'll be there for the being there stuff, and we'll be there for you to also throw abuse at after you've finished this book... because we're positive we'll get some.

But... big but... as with The Escort series... we have plans y'all! Everything happens for a reason. Things had to happen this way.

Trust us ;)

Or don't, because clearly, no one is safe...

Get the double meaning? Teehee.

Let's thank all the people... although Brunette is usually far better at that than me :) She's my superstar DJ and I'd be lost without her. Well and truly. She's my sister from another mister, my partner in devious written crime, and I love her.

David, our fabulous editor, the one who makes our words prettier... never leave us. Although at the time of writing this, he hasn't read the ending of this book yet, sooooo...

Sarah, Hilary, Zoe, you absolute magical humans, you! They alpha'd the shit out of this and you're also never allowed to leave us, despite the heated comments ;)

Sam, we ask a lot of you, and you stay on our arses like a fly on shit and we love you for it! Our newsletters would be wank without you.

Kirsty, at the Pretty Little Design Co, your cover designs are friggin' spectacular as usual! Our cover model, Sabrina Marzano (one of Blondie's Am-Dram friends!) thanks for being our badass J. Chris Brudenell, photographer, he's amazing to work with!

Every single reader who picks up our books, thank you for taking a chance on us! Please show us some love and leave reviews/stars, spread the love and come join our book group for random fun!

Because who doesn't love random fun?

Details to follow... :)

THE BRUNETTE ONE

Geeeesh, how am I supposed to top that?

I will say this, One Kill was always supposed to exist and very quickly, the ending was the one you read. We admit that with The Escort Series, we were able to keep y'all in doubt for so long only because we had no idea who the Forever One would be for so so long.

But for J's story, it was clear from the start.

So, yes... you are angry and feel betrayed and some of you are screaming that you will never read us again...

Trust us, you want to read One Love because as much as we love to tear you apart, we love putting you back together even more.

Now, for the emotional shizz.

First, all my admiration and love goes out to Blondie. This summer was a difficult one, devastating even, and I can't imagine the pain and grief that she's going through right now. One thing I can say is that even in her own sorrow and ache, she is always here for everyone. Me, her family, her friends, our readers... every one. Her heart knows no bounds, it's a thing of beauty.

To David... shit dude, hope you'll forgive us.

Hilary, Sarah, Zoe... ***does her best Titanic Rose impression*** "Come back. Come back."

Sammy O'... yeah, we'd be lying in a fetal position, crying in a corner without you. I'm not even kidding.

Kirsty, Sabrina, J. Chris... we hope our words did your artwork justice.

To Candi Kane PR... thank you for working so hard for us and for helping us bring our stories to readers beyond our reach.

To you... Yes, you. There are no words to describe the feelings we get every time you post a review or make a comment on our posts or message us with your thoughts on our books. It's like a shot of adrenaline that keeps us hyped up for the next book. Without you, there wouldn't be much of an "us" so... THANK YOU.

Thank you for reading, thank you for reviewing, thank you for letting us know that we exist, rent free, in your filthy mind.

BOOKS BY N.O. ONE

Dark Romance

The Escort Series (MF)

The Rich One ~ https://geni.us/TheRichOne

The Kinky One ~ https://geni.us/TheKinkyOne

The Filthy One ~ https://geni.us/TheFithyOne

The Broken One ~ https://geni.us/TheBrokenOne

The Almost One ~ https://geni.us/TheAlmostOne

The Forever One ~ https://geni.us/TheForeverOne

KOK (RH)

Kings of Kink ~ https://geni.us/KingsOfKink

The Reapers Mafia Crew Duet (MF)

One Kill ~ https://geni.us/TheReapers1

One Love ~ https://geni.us/TheReapers2

The Psycho Trilogy – Sons of Khaos (MF)

Psycho Hate ~ https://geni.us/PsychoHate

Psycho Love ~ https://geni.us/PsychoLove

Psycho Reign ~ https://geni.us/PsychoReign

Website & Newsletter: www.author-no-one.com

Facebook: https://geni.us/Facebookauthor

Facebook Group: https://geni.us/FierceReaders

Instagram: https://geni.us/Instagramauthor

Goodreads: https://geni.us/Goodreadsauthor

Bookbub: https://www.bookbub.com/profile/n-o-one

Linkedtree https://linktr.ee/n.o.one

BOOKS WE THINK YOU SHOULD READ

Dark Romance

DATE WITH THE DEVIL (MF) ~
HTTPS://GENI.US/DWTD

Contemporary

THE UCC SAGA

DISHEVELED ~ HTTP://AMZN.TO/2ARPBXP
DISARMED ~ HTTP://AMZN.TO/2MYVXNN
DISCARDED ~ HTTPS://AMZN.TO/2VWTRPF
UCC BOXSET ~ HTTPS://AMZN.TO/3LJVEPE

STANDALONE

THE WISH ~ HTTPS://AMZN.TO/2FTIKQB

Rom-Com

THE WOOLF FAMILY SERIES

SCREWED ~ HTTPS://GENI.US/SCREWED
SCREWED UP ~ HTTPS://BIT.LY/3IBFWKB
SCREWED OVER (COMING SOON)

Supernatural

SOUL GUARDIANS SERIES

REPRISE ~ HTTPS://BIT.LY/3CT9NPE

Eva LeNoir

Fun Flirty Romance

OTHER HUDSON INDIE INK AUTHORS

Paranormal Romance/Urban Fantasy

Stephanie Hudson

Xen Randell

Sorcha Dawn

Georgia Seren Mills

Crime/Action

Blake Hudson

Jack Walker

Contemporary Romance

Gemma Weir

Nikki Ashton

Nicky Priest

Jax Knight

Printed in Great Britain
by Amazon